# Wings
## *for*
# LEAH SPARROW

## TISHA COLE

xulon
PRESS

www.xulonpress.com

# TABLE OF CONTENTS

# INTRODUCTION

The world lives in color. It sees in color. It judges in color. The world, intentionally or unintentionally, overlooks that which is less than dazzling and flamboyant. So, for those who are not as colorful in the kingdom of life—animal or human—what of them? What is their part in life? The world has much to learn about that which is small and demure. It needs to see differently.

> *For who hath despised the day of small things?—*
> *Zechariah 4:10*

# DEDICATION

This is dedicated to the One I love--
*my* Aquila

To my loving husband, Gary,
so patient and supportive.
Thank you for believing in me.

To our beautiful daughter, Jessica,
you were born and, in me,
a heart to love so fully.

# Chapter 1

# SMALL BEGINNINGS

*For who hath despised the day of small things?*
*Zechariah 4:10*

"Yes, I'm quite sure she's the runt of the family," said the father of the brood, examining the last hatchling up and down with a careful eye.

The tiny birdling felt something of big size hover over her. She couldn't see it, but she felt it. A shadow cut her off from the bright sun's rays that pierced through the maze of branches and leaves. Now a new awareness to her wholesome beginning came—a little shiver.

"Out of all four of them, she's the tiniest."

"She might be the tiniest," mother whispered in awe, admiring the diminutive figure, "but she's so cute." Her head came close to her babe. "I'm naming her Leah. Leah Sparrow." Then, she added in a sad tone, "It means 'tired and burdened'. It'll be a hard life for her."

In the kingdom order of birds of flight there is a particular family known as the sparrow. In this immense family of sparrows is a clan named the Chipping Sparrow, and living in a world where names have the tendency to be a tell-all for its bearer, the Chipping Sparrow name does little to distinguish it outright. Yet, within its official identity is a more illustrious name: *Spizella Passerina*, a fine name which quickens thoughts toward portraits of feathered beauty and physique. But, sadly, the only endearing factor for this *Spizella Passerina*, this under-privileged little Chipping Sparrow, is its charming Latin name.

Songs from the bird kingdom enveloped nature in a chorus of melodies. Summer birds flew back to their breeding grounds to populate the earth; including the Chipping Sparrow that produced light-blue speckled eggs. It was on a day that shone with much warmth and promise, in a certain Chipping Sparrow couple's nest embedded in a crook of a tree limb, that a particular fledgling was born. She broke unceremoniously out of her oval structure, the last one of four eggs. And although she was already small as sparrows go, she was thrust into yet another position not of her own choosing: she was the smallest of them all.

An expanded world presented itself to Leah, but as the sun beamed down on her featherless body, a thin fleshy veil shielded her eyes. The unusual type of warmth compared to her egg shell felt good to her pale, bare skin. Hearing the wild sounds more acutely now that she was outside made her very curious as to what was going on around her; yet some of those sounds were very familiar to her.

"Well, she'll still have the Chipping Sparrow brown and gray feathers, the black lines running throughout her body, the chestnut-colored crown," father said, almost as a question, gently turning her over this way and that. "The tiny black beak, our whitish undersides?"

"Well, certainly she will," mother answered, smiling at her worried mate. She nestled tenderly on top of her brood. "She is one of us, after all."

The prophecy concerning her surname seemed to play out its part in Leah's life. She spent most of her energy fighting for every scrap of food that came to the four siblings via her parent's hunting. Being the smallest there was no choice but to take whatever was left, whether it was enough or not. Her parents weren't mean or negligent; food wasn't easy to come by when there were four mouths to feed. Nature ordained that they be fed every twenty minutes to survive, so the new parents were focused in constant flying mode.

"Mom and dad are back with food," Leah chirped. "I'm so hungry, my mouth is watering. I hope it's a good, juicy bug." But the larger gaping mouths and the bigger wobbly heads pushed her to the side in the ensuing mayhem. "Well, I guess I'll have to wait until next time... again," she said, a little sigh escaping her. She sat back down into her spot on the nest. A little growl sounded in her stomach and a strange thought about survival of the fittest raged in her spirit at another missed opportunity to satisfy her appetite.

The fledglings grew older and stronger, including Leah. Their soft fluffy coats gave way to the telltale feathers of brown and gray, now closer look-alikes to their parents. But, Leah noticed something a little bit odd about herself, and it seemed the others did, too.

"Why is Leah smaller than us, Mother?" Jayda asked. "Her colors are a little bit different than ours, too."

Before Mother could answer, Noey chimed in. "Because she was the last one out of her egg. The rest of us had first dibs on everything. Ha-ha!"

"Noey, that's enough," scolded Mother. "You're not being very nice about Leah's feelings. How would you like it if others said insensitive things about you?"

"I wouldn't like it very much at all, Mother," Noey said in a quiet tone. He looked down, swinging his foot back and forth methodically.

"Well, I'm glad you acknowledged that. Now apologize to your sister at once."

"Yes, Mother." He turned toward Leah. "I'm sorry that I hurt your feelings, Leah."

"It's alright, Noey. I forgive you."

"Now, Jayda, to answer your question," Mother began, locking a stern look on Noey to discourage him from speaking out again. "No one knows why things turn out the way they do. We can't control nature. But it in no way lessens the fact that Leah is one of us and that we all belong together as a family." Mother looked at her growing brood lovingly. "Does that make sense?"

Cale opened his mouth as though to add his own opinion for Leah's condition when he saw his mother's eyes bearing down on him. *Clunk!* He shut it quickly. The foursome nodded their heads in agreement, for they knew by their mother's looks that it was time to be still. But, the words already spoken formed more questions than answers in Leah's heart.

Unique changes took place as the baby birds grew. Flapping the two appendages on their sides gave them the sense that flying from their cumbersome nest was a closer reality. Starting out as little shivers allowed their muscles to grow strong for the ability to control their wings and be airborne in the wind.

The wind. They've all heard it before; that mysterious, uncontrollable force. They've seen it, too, though only as an invisible energy that curiously lifted their parents and other feathered kinsman, winged insects, countless lose leaves, and even wonderful aromas around them. On any given day the wind could blow so gently through the woodland as though afraid to unsettle floral petals before their time. But other days it might tear across the forest with such intensity that the birdlings feared for their lives; apprehensive of their nest sailing off the branch to touch down in a strange land never to be seen again. It was at times like these, huddled close and holding each other tightly, as the wind whooshed on all sides, that their trepidations outweighed any desire to fly at all.

The young sparrows found they could stand on their own two feet with a steadier stance now, jumping in eagerness as their parents returned with squirming food; protein for strong growth. The feistier ones discovered they could also wield their beaks as weapons.

"Ouch! Who poked me?" cried Leah.

"It wasn't me," said Noey, in singsong fashion. "I wasn't even close to you."

"Oh, yes you were, Noey, you little liar," Cale said. "When Leah had her back to you, you reached over and pecked her. I saw you."

"You saw nothing, Cale, and you know it. I'm going to tell Mother that you lied," Noey retorted. "You didn't see me do it, did you, Jayda? Tell him I didn't do it."

"Leave me out of this, you two," Jayda snapped. "I don't want to fight. It's crowded enough in here as it is. We've got to get along or it'll be hard on all of us."

"Well, I know I didn't do anything wrong," quivered Leah. "I'm the victim in all of this. I just wanted to know who did it, that's all."

"Oh, quit being such a baby, Leah," Noey sneered. "You always cry about everything."

"I do not."

"Oh, yes, you do. Ask the rest of them. You're afraid of your own shadow."

Leah turned to Cale and Jayda, expecting to be defended, but they both looked away, avoiding any eye contact. Leah hung her head. She scooted as far away from them as she could. It was hard thing to do in a nest that grew smaller every day they grew bigger.

"Now that their feathers have begun to grow out they are starting to look like our family clan," Father said with pride. "The Chipping Sparrow clan."

"Yes, they are," said Mother. "But, I've been noticing something a little bit unsettling, and the children have noticed it, too. Do you think Leah's coloring is somewhat duller than the rest of them? I mean, I know she's smaller, but her colors are not quite the same."

"Yes, I've noticed that, too." Father sighed. "And the world out there can be very cruel." The elder sparrow flew to the nest as the youngsters argued once again about space. "Settle down, children. I have something of legendary proportions to share with you."

The little ones stopped bickering with each other and stared at their father. Now curious, they shoved and bumped until they were comfortable enough to listen. He looked up at the sky and pointed to it. "Can you see all those stars up there? Well, listen very closely because in those stars is a story about you—your bird kind—that began a long, long time ago."

The tiny sparrows leaned forward with large eyes fixed on their father. Their mouths hung open in anticipation as he cleared his throat and began in a hushed tone.

"A caelis enarrari—the heavens declare. A miniscule mass called Thought floated in a sluggish manner in the vast black ink of the cosmos. Though this Thought was no bigger than the tip of a pine needle, it contained light, and could still be seen against the darkness. The Thought's deepest desire was to live and to move and to have its being, so it threw itself into action. Jetting throughout the galaxies, it collected enough stardust onto itself to make a noteworthy change and it began to grow; although in all comparisons it still remained smaller than a human's fist. Just the same, it was as strong an instrument as one. The significance of it all was that this Thought was now alive and its name was Spayro.

The now larger Spayro became conscious of an uncomfortable feeling inside of him: loneliness. There were no other lights his size, or ones that looked like him. "This is not acceptable to me. I need to search the universe for a soul mate. I wonder what would happen if I traveled faster than the speed of light?"

With desperation setting his course, Spayro geared up for the fastest ride he would ever embark on, now or ever again; for it could cost him his life. Speeding off, he torpedoed through the still, umbra universe creating a long stream of light behind him. It was so bright it could be seen for many space miles. Passing planet after planet, narrowly missing falling stars and tumbling pieces of meteors, he continued on, farther and faster. But, the longer the search continued the more his thoughts began to darken like the night around him.

"This is not good. I can't keep thinking bad thoughts about being alone. Those thoughts will extinguish all my light. There's got to be someone out there for me. I know I was not meant to be alone in this great cosmos."

But, hope began to fade and so was his light. He lost more and more speed. Then, something happened that altered his thinking. He heard a sound unlike any other sound; a sweet melody, and it came from across the galaxy. Spayro stared in the direction with renewed hope. Although he could not see anything as yet, he was as aware of it as much as he was aware of his beating heart. He smiled. Not understanding how he knew, he sensed the search was coming to an end; and it was just in time.

Confidence rallying him on, Spayro increased to greater speeds, zigzagging through the maze of space matter. His thoughts were fixed toward that one light, the one he knew he'd recognize when he saw it. Growing brighter at every stellar mile, hope had renewed his stamina.

"There it is!" Spayro saw a tiny pinpoint of light zipping toward him.

"Who are you?"

The question formed into Spayro's mind like a soft breath. Still a deep span of space away from each other, their impressions touched gently.

"My name is Spayro." His heart was at his throat. "What's your name?"

"My name is Chippy."

Spayro noticed the tenderness in her thoughts toward him. His heart beat as fast as he was flying for he knew that this light would be his soul mate forever. The end. And that, children, is how the courtship of the first Chipping Sparrows began," Father said with satisfaction.

"Wow, Father, that was the greatest story I've ever heard," exclaimed a small voice from the audience.

"Yeah," chimed the little birds, awestruck by their gifted storyteller.

"Well, that's the celebrated legend about our clan and our great beginning, young ones. That's how it was told to me by my father, and how it was told to him by his father, and so on and so forth."

"But, what happened after they met, Father? How did they come down here to earth?" Leah asked. "You just can't let an important detail like that slip away. You just can't."

"That part of the story will come at a later date, young lady. It's time to go to sleep. Good night, children," he said to the disappointed offspring. He flew to a nearby branch as his family settled down for the night.

Leah picked up a pine needle stuck to the nesting material. She raise it toward the sky, spied an opening in the trees, and matched its petite point to a glittering star.

"Wow. To think my ancestors began as small as the tip of this pine needle," she whispered. Leah let out a tiny hum as she thought about that. She couldn't wait to hear the rest of the family mystery. She stared into the black, star-studded night again. Height beyond measure loomed above the forest trees; that place where strange and wonderful things dared to happen as was told by her father.

"Oh, it's so comfortable here," Leah murmured as she snuggled under her mother's body for warmth. She felt safe and sound, that is, until her brothers and sister began squabbling again.

"Get out of my way, Jayda," yelled Cale, the oldest. "You're in my space."

"I am not," she yelled back. Jayda was the second oldest. "You're the one that's in *my* way."

"Both of you are in the way!" screamed Noey. "You're as fat as the cows in the meadow mother talks about…and you're squishing me out of the nest. Move!" he grunted, as he shoved his way around.

"Be still, all of you," Mother scolded. She shifted, looking down on them. "It'll be morning soon. A different kind of day is ahead for all of you tomorrow. So be quiet and get some rest."

Physically settling down was not easy for the sparrow youngsters with what was going through their minds. Whispers ensued as to what their mother meant when she said "a different kind of day." What was going to happen? The little ones, tightly fitted into the nest (one of them in deeper protest than the others), now stirred with a different excitement. But only for a short while as the coziness of their mother's body helped them fall asleep quickly.

Mother breathed in a deep quiet sigh. There was pain in her heart. It was time to teach her children how to fly. It was time to let them go.

"We're learning how to fly today?"

The sparrow fledglings cried out their surprise as high emotions ran through each of them. Leah mostly felt the emotion of fear mount even as she watched the other three almost jumping out of their skins with excitement. She wasn't so sure what to think about this new turn of events.

Learning how to fly did present a new challenge for Leah, wondering if her size would give her any problems. Cale, Jayda, and Noey were the first to attempt the daunting jumps off the tree limb, though it took Noey a little bit longer. Almost toppling off the branch on the first try, Noey was allotted an extra day before trying it again. Leah nearly choked witnessing her brother's near fatal fall. She cowered into the nest, her wings covering her head, until the flying lessons were over.

"I can't look," she whimpered. It only deepened the fear whether she would ever conquer the world of flying. But, her parents were not allowing her any extra time to get prepared.

"Leah Sparrow, it's high time you got out of the nest," exclaimed her mother. "You can't stay in there." She pointed outward with dramatic flourish. "Your destiny is out there in the world just like your sister and brothers, just like your father and I did before them."

"Yes, Leah. Where would we all be if we didn't leave our nests? You've got to stir up some boldness in you, girl, and try out your wings."

"But, Father, Mother, I don't think I can do that."

"Nonsense," Father grunted. "It's the most natural thing for a bird to do. Just start by climbing up on the rim of the nest, out to the branch, and...and...jump!"

Leah looked at her father, bewilderment clouding her eyes. *Is it really that easy?* she thought as her eyes swooned looking down from her place of safety. She was the last of the siblings to attempt even the shortest move: climbing onto the rim of the nest. But, onto the limb? Leah trembled as she studied the long, narrow branch that would either be her step to true freedom or, as she witnessed of poor Noey, a close misstep to a fast way down.

Matters did not help when she overheard worried whispers. "She could have trouble flying. She didn't show that same fighting instinct inside her like her brothers and sister did." "She doesn't fight for her food like the other children do." "She doesn't exert her wings with much enthusiasm. These are basic survival instincts for a bird. It's for her very life."

Memories of her mother flapping her wings in front of them, when they were tinier, flashed before her. Remembering the fingers of air touching her face electrified her body, stirring up her little spirit. An understanding came to her at that exact point of contact: the importance of flying. It was a necessary element, and it was also beautiful.

Deep down Leah wanted to please her parents; to be with her brothers and sister who were enjoying new life outside the nest. She could be flying with them all through the woods. But, it was hard to fight against doubt-filled words that plagued her thoughts, especially when she was expected to sail off a high platform and to remain up. She knew her parents never intended any negativism to harm her; they were only concerned. Yet, fears were born from those words; fears that the world was a cruel place and that it was out to get her.

"I think I'm destined to be all alone here in the nest," Leah lamented.

# Chapter 2

# IT'S A CRUEL WORLD

*Cruelty is fed, not weakened by tears.*
*-Plubius Syrus*

Leah did learn to fly. Under her parent's patient and loving guidance, she climbed step by step out of the nest and onto the limb, ever closer to that final stage she dreaded. Though that first attempt was only a short spurt, landing her only a couple branches lower from where she began, Leah was elated.

"Yes-s-s!" she squealed, lifting her wings up over her head in triumph like an Olympian athlete. "I did it! I did it, Mother and Father."

"Yes, you did, Leah," said Father with a smile. He hoped it wouldn't end there. "That's the way to do it. Now, try it a little farther and before you know it, you'll be on your way just like the others."

Leah steadied herself once again and, with one long intake of breath, she plunged into the air with opened wings and flew away from the tree for the first time. It was no small surprise when she realized how far she traveled this time, but quickly decided to land on a branch before further realization sunk in.

"I did it again! It's really not as hard as I thought. It's just taking that first plunge that's the scariest." Her mother joined her, swiftly and easily. "I'll be as good as you soon, Mother."

"Yes, you will, Leah. We're so proud of you," Mother said with a laugh. She heard Father heave a big sigh of relief on the next branch. She smiled. "Now, Leah, we have to go down to the ground so I can show you how to find food."

"Wha-a-at?" Leah's eyes widened with panic. Thoughts more frightening than flying barged into her mind. For the first time in her life she would come in contact with the ground, with touching the earth, that uncertain solid realm way below her nest of comfort. She's heard strange things about it before. Mother and Father divulged information to their little ones about other kingdoms of non-flying entities that traveled the browns and greens of nature. She was aware of squirrels, chipmunks, and other furry four-legged creatures that lived in their woods. Her thoughts were brought back to the present by her mother's tender prompting.

"Leah, this is just another step to growing into who you are as a bird. Everything will come to you naturally."

Staring down to the faraway ground, she closed her eyes and, like a prayer, quietly repeated, *I can do it. I can do it. I can do it.*

"Alright, Mother," she said, haltingly. "I...I can do this, too."

"Yes, Leah, you will conquer this, too."

Mother flew to the ground. She checked around and gave a commanding chirp to Leah.

Leah could barely see her mother, so tiny from the perspective of a tall tree, so camouflaged by the natural surroundings. She understood the insurance of height; not much came to attack them in a high perch. But, that vast wilderness below her? It was about to become a bigger world—good and bad. Yet, with all the uncertainties Leah was experiencing, she remembered her sibling's path of success and felt a spark of encouragement surge into her spirit.

"One, two, three-e-e!" With thumping heart, Leah glided towards the ground. She felt the downward plunge come a little too fast, but instinctively, she used her wings for better lift to slow her down. Still, she bumped into her mother in the landing. "Oops. Sorry, Mother, I guess I didn't have it under control like I hoped." She let out a nervous chuckle, thankful that they were both in one piece.

"That's alright, Leah. The fact that you're down here and not still in the nest is a great relief to us. You had us a little worried, child. But, it's all turned out very good."

Mother signaled for the next step at hand and began pecking the ground, immediately finding seeds and bugs to place into her youngster's mouth. Leah's body shivered with energy, ballooning her soft little feathers outward, as she waited for a morsel of food.

The realization came to her that soon she and her parents would part ways. This bittersweet moment spent with her loving and attentive mother was a true fact of wildlife. She would soon come face to face with a whole New World all by herself, leaving behind the things she had grown to love.

The long days of summer took Leah to new grounds. She discovered the two-legged species called humans and became familiar with them as they worked in the fields, hearing the rattle of machinery rumbling down the long range of land. Faint sounds of human language drifted through the air from neighboring farmhouses, crossing fields and yards, echoing imperceptibly from porches as the welcomed rest came after a long hard day.

Leah noted a peculiar connection between man and beast as various domesticated animals grazed in large pastures, peacefully filling up on luscious grassland. But, one thing most interesting to her was a unique manner of understanding between humans and birds. Quite unexpectedly she found many homes welcomed her kind to their backyards, opening a plethora of seed havens for birds to feed to their heart's content. Life became a little bit easier as she filled up on a variety of seed.

On her own for a few months now, Leah sat thinking about the strange transformation in her life in such a short time. Gone were the days with her brothers and sister, her mother and father. Only sweet memories of being a tiny birdling requiring care remained in her heart. She built her nest in a woods situated between two large fields far from the homes she visited when her palate hungered for a taste of something else other than the crunchy crickets or juicy caterpillars. She loved this wooded area. It would be her promised land every spring soon after the last bit of winter spent itself over the territory.

Leah encountered many from her clan, the Chipping Sparrow, and countless other distant cousins throughout her travels. She noticed how distinct they all really were, as though noticing them for the first time. Her clan was one of the smaller versions of the sparrow families, although not by much. There were other clans with distinguishable colorings, a chosen few with noteworthy songs, and even some with temperaments quite divergent from clan to clan. She reflected on it all, and then she compared. A dramatic shift took place in her life like water in a closed pot with wood continually fed into the raging fire and, as pressure builds up, the steam can no longer stay put. It must burst out, hot and furious.

"It just isn't fair," Leah said with anger. "How can there be so many sparrows and so many clans, and I have to be the one that looks like this? So drab!"

Not forgotten were the hurtful things her siblings voiced about her size and color. Though it saddened her, she really didn't know what the fuss was all about. She had her mother to look after her, to defend her. But, now she was alone; alone at the feast gardens where hanging feeders packed with delicious seed awaited hungry aviaries and some less then friendly distance cousins who marred those visits for her. Though they spoke face-to-face to her, they said more behind her back.

"Look at Leah," whispered one of them. Her name was Dara, a Song Sparrow. Two others with her turned to look, and quickly turned back, their shoulders quivering as they sneered. "What do you think, cousins? She hardly looks like her own clan."

The Song Sparrow was a beauty. She wore deep, rich streaks of browns against a whitish underside which gave her a look of elegance. With a lovely shade of slate gray striping a rufus-shaded crown, she easily stood out from among her peers. She also possessed the ultimate in a bird's most natural appeal: she was an exquisite songstress. With a song consisting of short clear notes followed by differing lilts and ending in a trill, it was a sweet song card for setting this sparrow apart from the rest.

As Leah eyed the Song Sparrow it took everything in her to keep from spitting out in frustration. She knew her own singing did not even come close to comparing. *Yes, I know Chipping Sparrows have a song of sorts, if I can call it that. But, it's all on the same pitch. Why broadcast that? Why didn't our ancestors have better imagination then this in music? They certainly didn't put much thought into it.*

With a smug look on her face, Dara approached Leah. "Where have you been, Leah?" She cleared her throat, "Hiding from the rest of us?"

"Hello, Dara," Leah said in a low tone. She knew her cousin's mocking behavior. "No, I haven't been hiding. I've just been at other gardens where I can enjoy eating with my favorite cousins." Leah quickly flew off to the farthest part of the garden, leaving her cousin behind with a scowl on her face.

"I can't stand it, the whispers, the teasing. Why don't they just leave me alone?" Leah fed on the seed scattered on the ground, though it left a bitter taste in her mouth. The sour thoughts deepened a wider gap between her and the rest of the world. "To top it all off, they happen to be right. She is prettier than me, there's no doubt about that." She felt a little burst of wind rustle her feathers. Turning, she saw a sparrow land next to her. It was another distant cousin, a House Sparrow.

"Hi. What's your name? Mine's Hoozer. I haven't seen you around here before, but, then, there's so many of us maybe we did and forgot. Haha!" He seemed an exuberant fellow that couldn't help rousing whatever was around him, no matter the situation. Leah only stared, not sure what to make of someone that talked too much. She went back to eating. "I just came in from the meadows. Boy, you can tell the snow's going be flying soon and there's going to be less food out there. That's why I come here. You know, this is one of my favorite garden feast areas. Don't you think it's great? I mean, it's got a little bit of everything. A lot of my favorites, that's for sure. What's your favorite? What do you come here especially to eat?"

Hoozer stopped. He realized he was doing all the talking. Studying Leah as she scratched the ground without any real effort, he said,

"You're so quiet. Did I do something wrong? I'm sorry if I did. I'm not sure what I did, but I'll apologize if I have to. There's no reason for something bad coming between two sparrows that just met and..."

"Be quiet for a moment and maybe I can say something, too!" Leah let out a big puff of air in frustration. Then, closing her eyes, she slowly inhaled and slowly let it out. Even though he had a frustrating manner of talking too much, Leah could tell he was friendly. He was a juvenile bird like she was. As a young bird in need of knowing her place in life, Leah thought that his friendly manner might be what she needed to help her find some common ground with him, even though they were from different clans.

"I'm sorry...uh... Hoozer, right? That wasn't nice of me. I just had a run in with those busybodies over there," she said, gesturing with a nod to the group which had grown to six gossips. "That's all. It didn't have anything to do with you."

Hoozer looked at the group, then back to Leah. He frowned.

"Why did you let them bother you...uh...sorry, but I still don't know your name."

"It's Leah. Leah Sparrow."

"They're just a bunch of losers, Leah. You shouldn't let them get to you. Whatever they said, I'm sure they don't know what they're talking about, anyway."

"I don't really want to talk about it, Hoozer. You wouldn't understand anyway." To change the subject, she said, "Hey, you're right, I've been noticing that winter's just around the corner, too. Are you ready for it?"

"Yea, I guess so." Not sure if he would be accepted by this little brown bird, Hoozer tried one more time to help snap her out of her stale attitude. "Well, Leah Sparrow, I'll stay here and keep the home fires burning until you get back next spring. But, for now" he added with exuberance, "there's still plenty of feast gardens for us to enjoy. You want to go with me?"

Leah looked at the strange bird. A warm feeling flooded her heart as she realized he was working very hard to make her feel better. She smiled at him. "There sure are, Hoozer. Let's go. We can head to one of my favorite places, the one with the two apple trees."

"Good! We can catch some of the last few bites this summer before winter sets in."

Both sparrows flew out of area and headed toward the landmark apple trees and the feast awaiting them. The back and forth conversation floated away behind them in the cooling afternoon. Leah felt better. She could forget the uneasy feelings she harbored back there. She would leave them behind so that she could enjoy the company of a new-found friend—Hoozer.

# Chapter 3
# THE VOICES

*The flowers appear on the earth;*
*The time of singing of the birds is come*
*And the voice of the turtledove is heard in our land.*
*-Song of Solomon 2:12*

The last of the bitter March winds spent themselves over the land and a new interval emerged with a sign: returning geese. Loud continuous honking traveled easily through the lifting currents as they moved with flawless ease across the bright sky. It was with high hopes that these long-necked wonders pulled an invisible veil of warmth behind them, ushering in the warm rains for the season's spring flowers.

Smaller summer birds came back, too, including Leah Sparrow; flying in the same wind, feeling the same sun, and hearing the same flight song. But, Leah wasn't interested in the spring's new melodies yet. Hunger pulled at her; to fill her stomach with food was a high priority. Although fully grown in size, Leah was not yet fully developed. She was only a yearling and her feathers had not yet procured the final stage of adult colorings that would evolve into that uninspiring grayish-brown tint she abhorred with a passion. It would also be another space of time before her crown would totally develop into its true color; something she had no control over. With a piteous sigh, Leah sat on a leafless maple at the edge of the woods and glanced around. Many other maples stood like sentinels, fixed in place for decades. She studied small droplets of sap dripping into weather-beaten buckets that hung around the rough, scaly trunks. She focused onto the dark ground below and let out a groan.

"Yuck. It's all so drab around here. So-o-o drab." A familiar darkness covered her face. "Just like me."

Wounded thoughts took her to a long ago memory; words spoken about her in a nest where four little birds broke into new life. Though they were not words spoken with evil intent, they were unwise words, nonetheless, which played a large role in her life almost as much as eating food. She could not come to terms with the way she looked different or even felt different, compared to the rest of her family and clan.

Leah spied animal tracks leading to a particular spot. Spreading her wings, she jumped off the branch with ease and flew to a lower branch for a closer look. She saw the telltale split-hoof prints of a deer. There were also tiny tracks of field mice on the patchy snow and traces of a rabbit's long, sleek hind feet. All tracks led to what was left of a wayward cob of corn from the last harvest. The larger forest creatures had dragged it to the edge of the field to eat the kernels in safety. The smaller animals gleaned what was left behind.

Leah looked around for any danger signs, and seeing nothing out of the ordinary, she flew down for a meal. Some of the kernels were finely cracked just as she preferred, thanks to the obliging help of the stronger-toothed beasts. She ate unhurriedly, but with a watchful eye.

A slight movement on a tree only a short distance away caught her eye. A fat gray squirrel sat on a thin branch eating from his secret stash. Well camouflaged by the tree's dull color, Leah would have missed it if it hadn't moved.

"Huh. He's pretty drab, too." Then, with angry heat covering her face, she added, "But at least he's got a beautiful plume of a tail that stands out more than anything I've got."

Suddenly, an intense cold breeze swept past Leah catching her off guard. Hearing something above the wind, coming through the abrupt swishing noise, she looked around.

*Yes-s-s. So-o-o drab. Jus-s-s-t like you.*

The wind stirred up a dirt-devil of corn, leaves, and twigs, swirling them along the ground and engulfing her in its path. Startled, not thinking fast enough to fly to safety, she partly ran, partly flew along the ground and ducked underneath a nearby thorn bush for protection. She quickly scanned the area from her hiding place, breathing heavily.

"What in the world? Was it just the wind or did I really hear something else?"

Her thoughts were all jumbled like the debris on the ground. The morning sun still shone as her eyes struggled to focus eastward. Leah waited until her heart and thoughts quieted down before she felt safe enough to leave the area.

In search of small twigs, grass, and dried leaves, Leah set out to build her nest home. She flew to nearby farms where chickens and ducks roamed, helping herself to small tufts of feathers scattered on the ground. She found a special prize: a long piece of string intertwined in a bush. Leah constructed her cup nest on the limb of a white pine standing close to the center of the woods. This wooded area housed many generations of sparrows, including the Chipping Sparrow, and though she had not run into any of her own family, there were many other clans already arriving from their winter home.

The area was a large secluded patch of trees, brush, and vines thriving in the shadows of nature, well away from the goings-on of everyday life of the human world. Only during certain times of the year were occasional voices heard close by, along with the rattling of farm machinery. With bulky oaks, cottonwoods, and evergreens, the woods would cloak Leah from many intruding elements.

But, this small wood held a greater treasure only a few yards away from her tree. It was a fishpond. Leah immediately liked the pond, a spot where she encountered and welcomed a chorus of high-pitched peepers and croaking frogs as though they were hailing her return to the territory. Soon the incessant shrills of crickets and cicadas would be joining nature's musical around her, too. Thirsty, she dropped down to the edge of the pond for a drink. The stillness of the water made a perfect reflection. Bending over, she saw her image very clearly.

"Yep," she grumbled. "I...am...a...sparrow." Staring at herself in the water, the portrait of a certain distant cousin came to mind: the White-crowned Sparrow. Its head was covered with black stripes on pure whiteness and its bill was an exquisite orange color. They stood out most handsomely of all the sparrow clans. "Look at me!" Leah cried out at her image in the watery mirror. She spread her wings out in despair. "It's not fair. I have no color, no distinguishing birthmarks, and my beak is black. Why couldn't I have been more like...."

"Hello-o-o!"

The loud voice came so suddenly that it sent Leah out of her depressive self-study and hastily up onto a tall thin sapling. From a safe distance, Leah looked far below. Ruffling her feathers, she let out a shrill screech.

"Hoozer, that was a dirty trick!" Leah directed her anger to herself as to her cousin for neglecting to stay alert while she was by the pond. It could have meant her life had it been an enemy.

Hoozer laughed out loud. "Sorry, little Leah, but I couldn't resist. You looked so out of it, I just wanted to have some fun with my little cousin."

"Well, it wasn't fun, Hoozer, and you can also stop calling me *little*," she scolded.

"I'm sorry."

She flew back down to the ground with frustration graying her face. *It's just like him; taking everything so lightly. Why shouldn't he? He's not the one that was terrorized.*

"What do you want, Hoozer? Did you come here just to bug me?"

"I came to see you, Leah. Really. We haven't seen each other since you came back from your winter home. Again, I'm sorry I did that. I was only joking. You know I wouldn't hurt you."

Leah did know. He was a favorite cousin to hang out with and although she knew he was a cut up, he was also a good friend. But he could irritate her, too. She eyed him as he drank and indulged in a cool splash. This male sparrow wasn't plain looking at all. His deep browns allowed him to stand out easily. A steel-gray cap, a deep black beak, and lighter cheeks gave him a valiant look. Also, a rich black spot high on his chest distinguished him from her Chipping Sparrow colorings. Leah took note of it all.

Shaking the extra water off his body, Hoozer turned around toward her. "It's great to see you again, Leah. It sure seems a long time since we last saw each other, doesn't it? Of course, it was the winter season and you were down south." Hoozer stopped for a second as he stared at her. Her eyes had a far-away look in them. "Are you alright, cousin? You're looking so...sad."

Leah quickly brought her thoughts back to the present. "Huh? Why would you say that, Hoozer?" Leah chuckled. "I'm not sad." It worried her that the forced chuckle would give her away. She had no intention of sharing her inner battles with anyone.

"Well, I just haven't seen you around much at the feast gardens lately with the rest of us. I was just wondering if it was because of Shadow, you know, from last summer? What happened there unnerved us all."

Leah shuddered as she thought about Shadow, a black cat that lived at one of the seed gardens. She watched in horror as one of their bird-kind was snatched up and killed by the feline menace. She went there only if she spied the evil cat inside the house sitting at his window seat where his stares were considerably less threatening than his teeth.

"That devil Shadow can keep the garden all to himself, for all I care, Hoozer." The tone in her voice grew louder in a desperate attempt to sound brave. "But, I'm not going to let a crazy cat keep me from it if I want to go there. Yes, I still go to the gardens, but sometimes I would rather hunt alone for my food."

"Leah, it's a dog-eat-dog world out there, and everyone's doing the best they can. I know I am." Tired of his cousin's indifference, Hoozer shook the water off his body one last time. "I don't know what's gotten into you, Leah, but I hope you find out soon." He flew away without another word to her.

Leah's mouth dropped open. "What'd I do?"

Without a doubt she couldn't have felt more miserable than at that very moment. Her foul mood chased him away, and on the first month back from winter's break. Feeling ashamed that she treated him badly, a stream of tears flowed down her face.

"I don't know what's going on either, Hoozer. But I hope I find out soon, too."

# Chapter 4

# THE BLUE JAY

*Desire hath no rest.*
*-Robert Burton*

L eah was small and plain, and she felt it even more so today. Numbness washed over her in the cool gray morning sky. She pictured her own personal cloud hovering above her. One reason being the last awkward encounter with Hoozer. She tried to find him at all their usual places, but without any luck. Not knowing his whereabouts made her day even gloomier. Their friendship was a special one. It was never deemed that two birds of a different feather should fly together, but theirs was a discovery of something more. It was trust. They were alone in the world searching their own young paths when along the way they found each other. It was a mutual need for friendship, with a tiny bit of curiosity, which melded this uncommon twosome.

Leah let out a little huff. "He's obviously avoiding me. I'll just give him some space and then I'll ask my cousins if they've seen him. Somebody's got to know where he is"

Spring's first raindrops pinged lightly against the dried leaves still clinging stubbornly to the massive oak trees near her nest home. Hearing the low resonance of thunder far away, Leah left the warm nest to beat the brewing storm. Since her favorite foods of grasshopper, caterpillar, and beetles were not in season yet, her hunger pangs led her to a feast garden, though a safer one than where the black cat resided.

Soaring over cut fields, yellowed meadows and lonely country roads, Leah settled on the line of a high pole standing close to a familiar home. She looked up at the impending rain approaching from the west. Unseen thunder boomed across the sky as flairs of lightening manifested from behind the fast moving clouds. The garden stood under two widespread apple trees still absent of spring buds in the back yard of a large well-kept farmhouse. Leah's attention went to a human carefully walking down the steps toward the feeders. She became familiar with this elderly woman who spoke gently to the birds as she fed them, cooing low and gently like a mourning dove. Of course, it was hard to understand human language.

"Come, little birdies. *Chik-chik*. Come on, come and eat. There's plenty for all of you. *Chik-chik-chik*." After the seed was gone, the old human turned back to the house.

Gearing up to fly from her perch, Leah suddenly felt a stirring of wind around her. A flash of blue color passed directly overhead. She could tell it was blue; it caught the corner of her eye. Instinctively, she stopped. The dining bird-crowd at the feeders flew off in various directions with protesting chirps and screeches.

"It can only mean one thing," Leah whispered as she stayed put. "The Blue Jay has arrived."

Leah stared at the Blue Jay who now commanded the area. He was a huge bird. Screeching as he ruffled his cobalt-blue feathers, he scanned the area for his favorite pickings, his blue-peaked crest standing out like a trophy. The only ones who remained were some feisty chipmunks and a squirrel. It was useless to even think about going near the food now, but that was fine with Leah. All she wanted to do was keep out of sight and observe the large impressive bird. Shrieking periodically to intimidate intruders, the Jay continued gobbling black sunflower seed. Leah flew into thick vine cover for closer observation.

"I've heard Jays are not friendly, can't be trusted. They ransack nest homes of small birds; eat their eggs, and even the young. I just can't believe that kind of vile behavior from some birds." But Leah still couldn't help being curious about the Jay. "They're so bold. Why can't I be that way? I would give anything to have that beautiful color, too."

The Blue Jay, full of seed, prepared to leave. Leah then saw an incredible thing happen. A feather detached from the Blue Jay as he went airborne. It cascaded down in a graceful, free-fall motion and settled down close to the feeding area. A crowd of waiting birds converged once again onto the ground to continue their interrupted meal. Leah waited for the right time, keeping an eager eye on the wayward feather. Her mind worked fast as she thought about the miraculous find. She flew out of her hiding place and landed close to the feather where it lay. Carefully and quietly she picked it up.

"What are you doing?" asked a small, chipper voice.

Taken by surprise, Leah jumped back and dropped the feather, but quickly stomped her foot over it. A little Chickadee flitted around her, pecking at the seed, and looking up at her in rapid succession.

"What are you doing? With that feather?" At every flurry of words, the tiny bird hopped to a bit of foliage for a bug, or swept up onto a high birdfeeder, then back again to poke at the ground.

"You mean this Jay feather?" Leah's head turned back and forth, up and down, to keep up with him. "I was just sort of thinking about taking it to my nest. I could use this feather and..."

"Oh, that Jay!" the Chickadee broke in, totally ignoring Leah's reply. "He gets me...so mad." The little bird ruffled his feathers in protest. "Who does he think he is? Crashing on everybody. He's so rude." Never stopping, the excitable little bird flew onto the suet feeder, then down to Leah again. "Makes us all wait. He gets his fill. We wait."

"Well, no," Leah said, cranking her neck to follow the Chickadee's quick moves. "It's just that Blue Jays are big and bold. We smaller birds aren't brave like that, that's why they irritate us." She added daringly, "But I sure wish I was that bold."

"Bwhot?"

Leah jumped and turned to see a female Robin with a fat squirming worm in her beak. The Robin dropped the condemned food and squashed it under her foot. She noticed the Blue Jay feather under Leah's foot. Rarely did a Robin come near to a feeding station like this, preferring open yards instead. The Robin bobbed her body up and down, showing off her prominent red-orange chest, keeping a close look out for any enemies.

"What?" she asked again. "The Jays are loud, obnoxious, and rude. What would a little sparrow want with that? The very idea."

"Loud. Obnoxious. Rude. They sure are." the Chickadee conjectured, still busy moving and eating.

Leah felt pressured. "I don't want to be loud and obnoxious, but I wish I was bold like... like..." Leah's voice trailed off. She watched the Chickadee flutter away before she could finish her sentence. At the same time, the Robin picked up her wiggling cuisine, harrumphed at Leah, and flew away, too. "Talk about rude!" she yelled after them. "I'll show them."

But, her anger didn't last long. The wind blustered around her. The morning's ominous bleakness had reached the farmhouse and the hanging feeders were now swaying like pendulums. Rain-filled clouds covered the sky with the swift assurance of a torrential downpour. Leah was the only one left at the feeders. Thunder boomed as big drops of rain pelted the ground, sending a mixture of mud and water up into the air. A little shiver ran up her back.

"I've got to get back home…now."

Picking up the feather, Leah flew off in the direction of her nest home. The sky darkened like a black cloak as the anticipated north-westerly drenched the soil. She was mad at herself for not heeding what was going on around her again. The deluge forced her to find shelter under thick, low-hanging branches of a pine tree. She would wait out the storm. Although she was wet, cold, and stranded, her spirits soared as thoughts of a long, blue treasure in her possession ran through her mind.

Travel came especially hard with the blue feather crosswise in her beak, but Leah made it back to her nest before the second outburst of rain came. Shaking the moisture off, she set her feathers back into place. An idea was born in her mind during the long wait in the tree shelter concerning the Blue Jay's feather: she would attach it to one of her own wings.

The feather was indeed the vibrant sky-blue that Leah had always admired from far distances. Now it was hers. From the quill tip upward, she examined the feather closely; the blueness flowed toward the top of the feather interrupted by a thin black line and ended with a bright white tip. Her eyes glistened with sheer joy.

"Yes, this is a fresh start for me, a new me," she said in a whisper. "I almost feel bold already just holding this feather." She placed it next to her own wing. "Wow. It's a lot longer than mine is. Well, I shouldn't be surprised. He is quite a bit bigger than I am. Now, let's see, how am I going to do this?" Leah studied the color again, comparing it to her own lackluster shade. She shook her head and clicked her tongue. "I know! I'll look for some of that thick, gummy sap that oozes out of pine trees and use it to glue the Jay's feather onto my wing. I have firsthand experience how sticky that stuff is when it dripped into our nest. Yuck. Well, it's crazy enough that it might just work."

The sun slowly peeked from behind the scattering rain clouds once again, and a smile snuck onto Leah's face. She flew off for the glue. The gummy resin seeped from a broken limb and with a small twig she scraped off a gob onto the tip. Waves of adrenaline shot through her at every beat of her wings as she flew back to the nest. The answer to all the misery she had been feeling was only a matter of a dip of glue away. Back in her nest, Leah took a long hard look at the Jay's feather.

"Well, the first step toward any change is always a huge one. This is my dream, but, oh my goodness, it's scary." Even as she held on to the hope that everything she planned would turn out good, she knew many unexpected things could happen. "Here goes," she whispered. Taking a few deep breaths to calm her nerves, Leah scraped a glob of sap with the quill tip of the blue feather. But, before she could decide what wing to place the feather, a peculiar noise caught her attention. Clutching the feather in her beak with the glob about to drip down, she heard the breeze through the pines. It was familiar to her, having lived in the evergreen forest; a continuous swishing sound ebbing and flowing at the impulse of the wind with the occasional eerie whistling coming through. But what Leah heard now was unique. The rainstorm had passed, yet it seemed a storm of another kind was brewing around her.

*Leah.* Barely breathing, Leah strained to catch what it was she heard. *Leah.* An oppressive rustling came icily through the trees. *Who-o-o are you? Who-o-o are you?*

"I don't want to hear this!" she moaned. Raising her wings up over her head she pressed them tightly against her head.

The wind finally subsided. Slowly lowering her wings, Leah couldn't hear anything. The normal goings-on of the woods continued as though nothing had happened. Wanting to keep busy, she continued where she left off, not wanting to dwell on the strange incident. Stretching her right wing out in front of her, the one she decided to adorn, Leah fastened the rich blueness on top of her brown ones. She situated it closer to her longer pinion feathers to better match their length.

"Wow." She stood very still so as not to disturb the glue. "Now for the drying part. Oh, I can't wait to see this tomorrow."

It was early evening now, the sun setting down easier than Leah was. She tried to stay calm, but the scenario playing in her mind won over the fear that had gripped her earlier.

"The glue will be dry by morning, and in the morning I'm going to the pond to see how the feather fits me, and, of course, how it looks on me, too. I can't wait!" she exclaimed. "Wait a minute. I'm too scared to look at myself. What if it isn't what I wanted after all? No, no, I have to see myself, regardless. Oh, I don't know what to think." Leah's ramblings did stop when a rather huge realization barged into her thoughts that made her shudder. "Oh…my…goodness. My new feather has to function well, too! I forgot about that. It'll be my first test flight to the pond, almost like when I took my first flying lessons as a babe-bird." Many firsts were presenting themselves to Leah in the coming break of dawn. "It's going to be a big day for me tomorrow…for a new me."

Leah shook her head vigorously, trying to shake off feelings of alarm from an unusual dream she had. She couldn't remember the dream, but she did remember there was something good happening today.

"The second the sun comes right through the trees and shines on the pond, I'm flying down to have a look at my blue wing."

Leah flapped her wings to get the feel of the newly added feather. Fear crept into her as it felt quite strange. But, flapping them a little bit harder, she felt more assured. She passed the first part of the test: the feather stayed intact.

The sun shone full and bright as it made its way over the horizon. Forgotten was the outburst of the angry rain clouds from the day before. The peepers around the pond had long begun their daily chorus and a young Mallard couple made themselves at home in the tall grasses by the pond. Flying into Leah's woods the day after she arrived, they made quite a fanfare of it. Duck voices are particularly noisome whenever they are riled up, and basically, any little thing could rile them up. So, Leah was sure that she would be entertained, and bothered, by their choruses throughout the summer. The bushes and trees were popping with buds as fast as the days were growing longer and warmer, adding hints of light green to the gray forest. Leah came out to the limb of her nest and ruffled her feathers vigorously. She elevated straight up a few inches from the limb to test the wing.

"Oh, good," she sighed with relief. "That part is taken care of. Now it's time to go inspect myself. Here goes nothing!"

She stretched her wings out and glided down to the pond, immediately feeling a slight pull to her right where she had bonded the feather. The wind cut ruggedly through the extra length of feather. Seconds later......

"Ouch!" She narrowly missed a plunge into the water, hitting the ground awkwardly. "That was close. I definitely have to refine my flying. There's more practicing to do."

Leah shakily moved to the water's edge. Turning sideways, she bent over to catch her reflection in the smooth water. There wasn't a ripple in the pond; she could see herself perfectly clear. The cobalt blue stood out like a slice of blue sky had spilled onto her. Next to her own brown and gray feathers, her shining ray of hope had become reality.

"Wow! I look like another bird entirely. I've got color now," Leah said, fanning her wing in and out a dozen times.

The Mallards sat in the water staring at Leah's strange doings for one being a bird. But losing interest, they went underwater with their tails tipped up in the air and yellow-webbed feet churning furiously as they retrieved plants to eat. Three box turtles lazily warmed themselves on a large branch protruding out of the cool water. Sunrays pierced through the trees like arrows, chasing away whatever muted shadows remained. As a shaft of light covered her, Leah basked in its warmth. She lifted her face toward the sun and let its caressing heat calm her shivering body. But what she was shivering about was puzzling her. After all, an exciting life lay ahead her. Yet the strange voices from yesterday were attempting to creep back into her mind. She shook her head.

"I don't want to think anymore. I have to go find some food. I need to eat."

# Chapter 5
# THE SINGER

*That which is not worth speaking, they can sing.*
*- Beaumarchais*

Leah spotted many sparrow cousins on the ground in front of a wide doorway of an antiquated barn; a sure clue that there was food. A couple of quiet pigeons kept close vigil as they stole pecks for themselves. Peeking over a worn fence, a heifer meticulously chewed with little interest at the variety of birds close by. Seed escaped from the farmer's bucket and onto the ground as he went about in the early morning to feed the animals, thus attracting the birds.

Leah flew down to the ground close to clans of White-Throated Sparrows and the American Tree Sparrows. She knew both groups were flying north to their breeding grounds. Landing a few feet away from them to observe their movements, she saw some cracked corn she wanted to get to before it was too late. Slowly, she made her way toward the feeding crowd. Leah picked up on their flight arrangements.

"Hey, American Tree cousins, we're heading on our way north. When are you going?"

"As soon as we're done eating here we're leaving, too, White-Throats, until winter."

"We're meeting up with the rest of our clan at a certain point and heading out. It's a long way to the tundra."

"Some of our clan already left a few days ago. We'll be not too far behind."

A White-Throated Sparrow spotted Leah. "Oh, here comes Leah, one of our Chipping Sparrow cousins. She probably just came in from her winter home."

"Hello," Leah said, in a light-hearted manner. To disturb their feeding sometimes meant trouble. They tended to be more aggressive then she was. Feeling the hunger pangs, she didn't want to be chased away while food remained. "How are you all doing?" She began pecking the ground. "I heard you say you'll be leaving soon for your great trip up north. I thought I'd come eat with you before you left." She gave them a too eager giggle. Only the one sparrow stopped to look at her, the one that noticed she had arrived, a White-Throated Sparrow. Leah continued. "Well, I guess we'll see each other again in passing, before winter begins."

The White-Throated Sparrow had a distinguishing bright white spot on her throat, an attractive black and white striped crown, and a most defining lovely yellow mark shadowing the top of her eyes. Nella was her name, and she was stunning; a most elegant bird of the sparrow families.

"What's this, Leah?" Nella had spotted the unusual blue object on Leah's wing. She seemed curious, wanting to inspect it more closely. Leah slowly backed away, unsure what to make of her cousin's sudden curiosity. "Do you know you have a strange blue thing hanging on your wing?"

"Well, yes, I do know. It's just a..."

Before Leah could finish her sentence, Nella reached out with her beak and tugged sharply at Leah's prized feather. "Here, let me pull it off for you."

Leah instinctively flew straight up off the ground and lunged at Nella with both feet, bowling her over. Letting out an alarmed cry, Nella scrambled to her feet. The cousin's shrill angry chirps set off total confusion everywhere. The pigeons instantly retreated and rushed out of harm's way.

With her pride hurt, Nella led a mob of sparrows in a chase after Leah who had flown up and through a large oak tree, down along the fence and then over the roof of the barn to escape their wrath. The posse kept rushing like a cloud of mad hornets behind her. She fled toward the meadow and away from the farm. Her new wing propelled her through the air quite erratically, but nevertheless, she raced for cover. Leah calculated that they would not follow her very far because of their scheduled departure.

She stopped on top of a rusty combine that stood camouflaged under over-grown brush and vines in a field far from the barn. The big machine resembled a prehistoric creature frozen in place with its conveyor arm protruding toward the sky as though reaching for one last breath before paralysis set in. Glancing behind her, Leah noticed that the posse had stopped following her, just as she thought.

"What in the world came over me?" she asked between deep breaths, incredulous of the action she had taken against her cousin. "Why did I react that way? I've never done anything like that before."

She sat on her haunches in the heat of the noonday sun. Insects flew passed her with their light droning sounds trailing behind. The long distant call of crows traveled distinctly through the light afternoon sky. She remained in a trance of thought about the whole strange interaction and her strange reaction. Was it really what she had wanted all along; to finally gain boldness and courage to stand up for herself? Did it really evolve from the Blue Jay's feather? But, a nagging thought barged through.

"I was angry! I attacked my cousin because I was angry. She probably just thought it was a wayward feather that got stuck on me and wanted to help pull it off. Why didn't I just explain it to her? Instead, I attacked her."

Still conscious of angry bird retaliators, Leah looked back toward the barn, but something else caught the corner of her eye. Something flashed across the sky, yellow-gold in color, like flowers she's seen growing on a trellis at a feast garden she frequented. It was the undeniable color of the Yellow Warbler, a songbird, flying toward the woods.

Leah held her breath. The Warbler was using her flight voice. Closing her eyes and lifting her head, she absorbed the lilting music. She sighed. For the few seconds she listened to the songbird there was harmony in her little corner of the world, especially after the vexing ordeal with her cutthroat cousins. It was a sweet alternative to the confusion that had been swarming around her like a hornet's nest. She listened to the sublime tune with total abandon.

"She probably has something special to sing about today. Maybe she's singing for a mate. It's so beautiful. I've always wanted to sing that beautiful, but my voice sounds about as welcoming as the crickets irritating chirps." Leah whined, "It's just not fair!"

Then a light sparkled in her eyes. "Wait a minute. If she's singing for a mate, she'll be in a good mood, and if she's in a good mood I can ask her for one of her feathers, and if I get one of her feathers…" Leah held her mouth wide open as revelation struck her. "I'll be able to sing that beautiful, too. I mean, the Blue Jay's feather helped me gain bold-ness. I just proved it at the barn with my cousin Nella. Why wouldn't the Warbler's feather help me sing better, too?"

Leah looked one last time behind her where minutes before irate sparrows were hunting her down. But, surely they had left for their northern breeding lands, forgetting about the lone little sparrow with the undisclosed blue object on her wing, the cause of all the commo-tion. Leah saw the sky empty.

"Whew! That's over with. Now, I've got to concentrate on that Warbler. I've just got to have one of her gold feathers."

With a new plan in mind, Leah quickly flew to the spot where the singer had entered the woods. Gone were the perturbing thoughts of the sparrow attack. Her head was now reeling with ways to approach the songbird. She hoped she could conjure up choice words to convince the yellow bird how much she could benefit by owning one of her feathers.

The singer had traveled deep into the woods, her song now barely a whisper. Though it was a brilliant day outside the forest in the clear afternoon sun, the now thickening woods blocked most of the daylight. Not familiar with these woods, Leah paid closer attention to her sur-roundings as she continued her search. All kinds of creatures traveled secretly in a darkened wood, whether for protection or for taking prey by surprise; something she wanted to avoid.

*There she is!* She could hear the singer again. *She must have stopped to rest.* Leah trembled with excitement as she settled down on a branch, straining toward the direction of the beautiful sound. As the bird crooned, Leah flew closer and closer, branch by branch, chirping her own call so as not to catch the other one by surprise. The last thing she wanted to do was annoy her flaxen benefactress. Unfortunately, the Warbler already bared an expression of indignation of one whose privacy had been encroached upon as she regarded Leah's arrival.

*Oh, no. She looks mad. But, I can't leave. It's the only chance I've got.*

The Yellow Warbler stopped singing in mid-chirp. Leah cautiously advanced within a few branches of her. Surprisingly, the vocalist did not move. Curiosity proved greater value than caution as to why a sparrow would dare come close to her. A cute plump bird, the Warbler sat staring at Leah with her prominent dark eyes.

"Excuse me," Leah began carefully with a sweet voice. "I don't mean to interrupt you, Miss Warbler, but I seriously need to talk to you, to ask you a question. That's all. That's why I followed you here."

The Warbler looked at Leah through narrowed eyes.

"Well, you did interrupt me, Sparrow, and in the middle of my song," she quipped with exasperation. She straightened herself up, inspecting Leah up and down. "I don't like to be interrupted."

Leah shrunk. Superiority exuded out of this talented bird that could sing exquisitely. Leah couldn't sing at all. The Warbler was a lovely yellow color; Leah was as interesting in color as the gray-brown mushrooms growing in the dank woods. Angered of how she was being treated, Leah still dared not say anything derogatory. She'd lose any chance of getting what she was after: a perfect golden feather.

"I swear, Miss Warbler, it won't take long. Please?"

The golden bird stared as though in unbelief of the persistent sparrow. Then she snapped, "Oh, all right. But, make it quick."

"Thank you." Leah made a mental note that it was the last time anyone would make her feel second-rate; soon everyone would look at her with admiration. "Miss Warbler, I've admired your beautiful voice for so long that when I heard you from across the field over there, I just had to come find you."

The bird continued looking at Leah with disparity, the oddity of it all keeping her fixed on her perch. She sniffed. "Well, go on."

"I'm small and plain with no singing ability whatsoever. But, I really believe all I need is one of your golden feathers to help me."

"Help you? Help you do what?"

"To sing beautifully, of course, like you do."

"Hmm," the little bird smirked. "First of all, I know it won't help you one bit. Secondly, giving you any of my feathers is out of the question, because I don't want to." She prepared to fly away.

Shocked, Leah blurted out, "Please don't leave!" Recoiling instantly, but with pleading in her dark eyes, she said, "I'm begging you. Can't you spare me just one?" The Yellow Warbler didn't answer. She once more made as though she was going to leave. "Please, miss. I need it for…my…other wing." Her words trailed off softly as she lowered her head. She didn't want to see the singer's face in ugly ridicule toward her.

"So, that's why you have that blue feather on your wing? What kind is it? Blue Jay?"

"Yes," Leah squeaked out. "I know you don't understand. You have everything going for you," Leah chuckled with unease. "You can't possibly understand why I'm asking you for one."

"No, I can't. A bird is born not made. Anyway, I've just preened myself and already took care of any loose feathers. I don't need to pull any more out, thank you."

Leah's eyes darted with excitement. "That's wonderful! Then, please, just tell me where you preened. That's all I ask."

With a dumbfounded look, the golden beauty eyed the little gray and brown apparition in front of her. One could almost detect a trace of sympathy for the sparrow.

"All right," she said, letting out a sigh of irritation. "I came from the rock hedgerow that stretches along between the forest and the adjoining field, about three big fields over that way. You should find some feathers there" This time, without hesitation, she flew away.

Leah let out a huge sigh of relief. She had almost lost this big opportunity. Quickly flying off the branch, she headed in the direction of the hedgerow feeling as light and bright as the sunrays that now beamed on her face. She broke out of the shady shroud of the woods and headed to where the singer pointed. Before long Leah found the rock fence and a smile of success crossed her face. *The feather is somewhere in this fieldstone and I am going to find it.*

Through the passing of time nature's strong elements had formed small valleys along its course caused by fallen rocks. Yet, it survived its long parallel existence, sporadically shrouded in vine outgrowths and scaled by tall yellowed grasses; a solid division between woods and land. An occasional bush towered past the fence with evidence of worn vacated nests lodged in their thin branches. Leah hopped along the fence, darting back and forth, carefully searching for any clue where the singer groomed her feathers. She stopped, resentment rising up inside.

"I wouldn't put it past her that she lied just to spite me and sent me on a wild goose chase." But, then, an exuberant bubbling of whistles farther down the stone barrier distracted Leah from her irritated thoughts. She watched a tiny wren swoop down and snatch a soft, yellow wisp of feather clinging to a bush. "Thank you, Mrs. Wren. Your search for nesting material helped me find the Warbler's preening spot." She flew to the bush and glanced down the wall to the ground. "Yes, there it is!" But, before she could make a move, the tall grasses along the rock wall betrayed that something was moving toward her. "Now what am I going to do? I can't get the feather not knowing what's down there." Leah made the dreaded decision to leave, for safety's sake, but before she did she took a quick peek over the ledge again. "That was a close one. I almost left my new feather because of that."

A tiny gray field mouse was rummaging for food, the reason for swaying grasses. Her eyes followed the little creature as it passed below her along the shaded wall. Leah carefully moved downward, branch to branch. With little space to maneuver between the bush's trunk and the rock wall, she painstakingly made her way closer to the target.

"I...can...do...this."

Leah liked to think she had outwitted the snobbish bird into giving her what she had asked for, and now here she was, inches from the prize. Finally reaching it, she picked it up.

"Ee-e-e-k! Ee-e-e-k!"

A terrifying high-pitched squeal reached Leah's ears. She knew it was a cry of distress. With the feather in her beak, she pushed hard against an indentation in the rocks to hide until she could look for a way of escape through the dense branches and shoots. Her heart was at her throat as she looked toward the pitiful sound.

Staring in shock and disbelief, Leah saw the little mouse she had seen only moments before now gripped firmly in the jaws of a large brown snake. Horror stretched across the face of the little rodent as Leah watched helplessly. Slowly and menacingly, the snake turned its head toward her. Icy, beady dark eyes glared at her.

Leah crashed through the tight branches and vines. She didn't care. Clinging tightly to the Warbler's feather, more out of confusion than possessing the mental capacity to get rid of the extra load, she burst through and made her escape as fast as she could move her wings — the one with the blue feather and the one awaiting the yellow-gold.

Leah was back in her nest and sitting low with her head down against her chest. Breathing heavily, she tried to stave off the fierce shaking of her body. Her mind swirled with the sequence of the day's events. The Warbler feather was still clutched in her mouth.

"If I hadn't seen the mouse first, if I hadn't waited and watched him go by me, if the feather had been closer to the area where the mouse was caught, if I was the one that was there instead of the mouse...if, if, if, if!"

Leah shuddered at the thought that she could have been the one in the snake's mouth instead of the unsuspecting mouse. Certainly she would not have been able to escape that tight space quickly enough; the mouse didn't. She finally dropped the feather.

"That poor little thing, it actually saved my life." She looked at the feather lying in front of her. Having admired the sun-colored object from far away, she felt anything but sunny now that she had it for her own. In the nest since the dreadful incident, her desire to do anything with the feather dissolved as fast as the sun went down.

The moon formed a perfect circle as the fading day gave way to the reaching fingers of darkness. It reflected onto the small pond through an opening between the trees, looking like a silver platter on a dark oval table. Watching the moon dance on the water's ripples caused by frogs lunging for a meal, Leah sat quietly, listening to the music of toads and crickets, feeling the breeze whisper softly through the pines and passed her nest. It was the balm that lulled her to sleep.

The early morning displayed a bright day ahead with no clouds, only a few short ashen wisps of night lingered momentarily in the western horizon as the sun began its ascent. An easy warm breeze blew in from the fields wafting in the full-flavored, earthy smell of freshly plowed ground.

Leah left her nest, not for food, but for new pinesap. It was time for the new feather to be glued onto her left wing. The painful thoughts of the previous day were gone as morning light fell on the new feather, reminding her that her mission must go on. It remained to be finished without regrets. Nature rained down good and bad on the animal world, nothing being able to escape its order of things. She flew along the edge of her woods and came across a snapped pine branch. Plenty of sticky sap oozed out freely. Leah found a small twig and, like before, scraped the ointment onto it and flew back to her nest.

Smearing the sap onto the feather's quill tip, Leah brought her left wing forward as far as she could. There was a two-fold reason this time for this feather: looks and balance. There was no denying she needed balance as much as she wanted enhancing. So, again, she sat still for the glue to dry to perfection. It was during this stillness that Leah's dream barged into her thoughts.

*Oh, I remember now. What a bizarre dream I had.*

But, wanting to rid the night's ghosts away from her, she immediately focused her sights on the morning activities around the pond. She needed distraction. The Mallard couple had built a nest, and the female was now incubating their eggs. Leah could hear the raspy yet soft uttering between the two ducks as they greeted each other. A turtle's head emerged from the water and remained like a statue for some time—perhaps waiting for the sun to warm the fallen tree drenched in moss so that it could climb up and warm itself.

A mother gray squirrel made a leafy nest in the massive oak directly across the pond from Leah's tree. She hunched rigidly on a branch of the oak, her fluffy tail curved expertly behind her back. Suddenly, with a steady back and forth flicking of her tail, she stood rigidly on all fours and began a rapid tirade of shrill protests. She was mad. Leah glanced down to see what was annoying the squirrel. It was a snake. It was swimming on the water and disappeared into an area of dried cattails bunched along the bank. Leah shuddered as yesterday's dreadful episode came back to her.

"Boy, it sure looks like the same snake I saw at the hedgerow yesterday. I hope it keeps slithering out of these woods and straight to the other side of the world." Leah quickly took in a sharp gasp of breath. "I remember my dream!"

*A shiny, round silver platter lay in the center of an oval table and right in the center of the platter was a little gray mouse. The mouse had a small bluebell flower attached to his right arm and a small yellow rose attached to his left arm. He was shaking profusely. The reason was directly in front of him: at the other end of the table was a large brown snake, its tongue flicking in and out with its unblinking eyes fixed hard on the small horrified creature.*

*The rodent frantically beat the small objects in the air trying to fly away from danger, but it was useless. No matter how hard he worked to move his 'wings' there was nothing he could do to quicken the process. He was stuck on that gleaming silver platter with nowhere to run. Whatever he tried to do, he managed only to skid on its slippery surface. The waiting snake began its effortless way toward the victim; an easy prey.*

Leah vigorously shook the ill effects of the dream from her body, but quickly remembered about the freshly attached feather. Afraid she had done damage, she checked it. It was still intact.

"Whew! I didn't want to go through that gluing process again," she said with relief. But, now she had another urgent issue at hand. "I've never seen a snake around here before. Now, what am I going to do for drinking water? What am I going to do when I need to look at my reflection?" She kept a close eye on the area the snake had disappeared into, scanning back and forth along the bank just in case it slithered back into the pond. "I'll have to be very careful about this until I'm sure that creepy thing is gone. Hopefully, it was just passing through." Then, Leah realized a worse situation. "Oh, no, the duck couple! They'll be having their baby ducks soon. I have to warn them." She was not going to let a repugnant snake help itself to tiny ducklings. With anxiety roiling inside, Leah quickly flew down toward the couple's nesting area. She forgot about the golden feather that was a part of her now. She forgot her rule to test the wings first.

It was too late. The balance she had hoped to gain was even more off kilter than before. The singer's feather was slightly shorter than Leah's, and coupled with the Jay's greater length on the other side, it left no streamline affect at all. The wind cut through the feathers quite erratically, causing Leah to fight harder than before to stay up. An alarming impression emerged that she could plummet to her death. Frantically, using her tail like a rudder, she maneuvered as best as she could to stay upright. But, to her horror, she was not heading to solid ground but toward the water. There was nothing she could do but brace herself for the inevitable.

*Leah.* A voice sounding like a breeze rolling softly into long meadow grasses whispered her name. *Leah.*

Her ears perked up. It distracted her for a second from the danger in which she found herself because, unexpectedly, everything seemed to slow down around her as though she was suspended in mid-air. Time seemed to stall in a slow motion vacuum, giving her life-saving seconds, delaying the grip of death a little longer. But, she also sensed something else just as abnormal happen around her. A tremendous swooshing sound came to her ears, a sound that only something of great size could make. The sensation of an incredible presence close to her brought chills. Dread of another kind gripped her. It could be a predator bird stalking her.

"This has got to be a dream! I've got to wake up!"

But, out of the corner of her eye, as she continued to watch the crash unfold before her in a bizarre warp of time, she saw something huge and shadowy make a sweeping upward motion beside her. Quite surprisingly, that shift caused a strong updraft to catch her underneath, propelling her a little higher and helping her drop safely onto the ground just in time. She landed with a hard thud onto soft green moss close to the water's edge.

"Ow." Leah lay, unmoving. Her mind reeled with rushing scenes of what had just happened, questions rushing in about what it was that just saved her life. She coughed. "That was too close. I would have died if I didn't get the help I did. What was it? It couldn't have been a hawk. I would have been its dinner. But I do know it was bigger than a hawk. And, yet, I'm alive. I...am...alive."

Leah's body was hurting, but it took second place to her elation of living through the flight and landing. She rested, breathing steadily, on the softness; a wet musty scent surrounded her. But, it was short lived. She sat up with a lurch and gasped. "The snake!"

She was nowhere near the area where the snake had entered the cattails, but Leah knew snakes travelled on the ground, also. She needed to check her reflection. After all, she just took the trouble of gluing the Warbler's feather. It must take precedent over her fear of being on the ground. She would just have to be more on the alert. Leah took a short wing's spurt off the bank and onto a waterlogged tree that had collapsed into the pond; now a landing for turtles, frogs, and an occasional duck to bask in the sun. She stooped over to look at her image. Her feathers were fairly rumpled from the almost disastrous flight. She groomed them down with her beak. Looking at her image in the water revealed a tiny tuft of her own feather sticking straight up from her crown.

"Huh. It reminds me of the crown on the Red Cardinals," she whispered. "That crest of theirs gives them quite an impressive look." Leah saw the little feather fall off her head and into the water. It was taken away quickly by small ripples. "Oh…my…goodness!" Another idea swiftly raced into Leah's mind. "I'll get a red feather for the top of my head just like the Cardinal's. I love how they look so grand and classy. And I will, too."

Leah brought her attention back to the water-mirror and looked at the two colorful feathers on either side of her body. They stood out like the sun's glistening rays on the water. But, though the feathers were lovely, Leah realized it only confirmed what she believed about herself.

"I'm just a plain nobody. A plain and drabby nobody," she mumbled.

Suddenly, jarring her thoughts, an onslaught of screeches cascaded down on her from high up on the trees. Cackling laughter penetrated the deepest part of her with its piercing din. Words formed in her spirit, ghostly words, hard to withstand.

*Fool! Fool! Never change! Never change! Plain Leah! Plain Leah!*

"No!" she shouted. "I don't want to hear it!"

The noise came from a band of crows. Leah stood mystified. How they had snuck into the woods without her noticing them was beyond her. Now departing with an eruption of wings and cries, the ink-colored birds bolted out. She shivered as the words echoed in her mind.

A painted turtle, done with basking, caught Leah's attention. She noticed the rippling effect of the water caused by its dive. Through the warping, she saw something moving above her head; something menacing. She quickly swung around. Hanging from a broken limb was a loose piece of bark swaying in the wind. She was on edge. The stinging words she imagined were working on her. Leah did feel like a fool. She almost died trying to fly down from her nest. This launching into an altered Leah with the latest feather could have caused her end. Yet, the reasoning of choice, once again, took over.

"I need another feather—a Cardinal's feather to help me look as stunning and prominent as any of the others in the bird kingdom. Just one more feather."

Almost losing life and limb and, incredibly, the occurrence that mysteriously saved her life was already forgotten. Another goal was set, and she was eager to begin. Leah smoothed down her feathers, settling the new ones deeper into her own so that flying would go a little bit more unobstructed. At least, that's what she hoped. Taking practice flights before leaving, she glided from branch to branch, climbing higher and higher, until she obtained the altitude she needed. Feeling more confident at each interval, she was satisfied she could make the distance. Her life depended on it.

# Chapter 6

# THE CARDINAL

*Trust, like the soul, never returns once it is gone.*
*-Publilius Syrus*

L eah flew as though on auto pilot heading eastward over plowed fields interested in only one thing—another feather. The newly attached ones were grasping much wind and keeping her from smooth travel, but steady focus on her next piece was enough motivation to keep going.

Below her an emerald patina blanketed the fields. A herd of horses raced across a meadow pounding the unyielding ground. Leah settled onto an area where many birds were entering and exiting a feast garden, a pleasant and familiar place to her. The two-story farmhouse included a screened-in front porch that faced south and a rounded tower that scaled up the side of the house, its gray-tiled roof extending into a peak. Topping the peak was a rusty metal weather vane in the shape of a running horse, noisily squeaking as a northwest breeze forced it to sway back and forth.

*Huh*, Leah mused, *a flying horse!*

She made her way to the back yard and the feeding station. News traveled fast within the ranks when seed was found at a human's feast garden. She saw a rabbit nibbling on tiny kernels overlooked by the birds. She spotted a swollen opossum braving the light to fill her body with nourishment for her coming litter.

Leah perched on a clothesline to observe the surroundings. Light-colored clothing swung lazily on the line. A fresh clean scent hung in the air, slowly stirring towards her. Hearing a low whirring sound coming up directly behind her, Leah twirled around in time to come face to face with a tiny hummingbird, its long sharp beak only inches from her face. It hovered around her for a few seconds and sped off to the opposite end of the clothesline. The diminutive bird was checking her out; a feeder filled with red nectar hung on a post of the clothesline. It was her space, her food. She was captivated by its beating wings since it was the first time Leah had seen a hummingbird up close; almost an invisible blur. The tireless marvel fed on the sweet drink, retrieving the contents with its long thin tongue.

"It's so pretty, so tiny," she whispered. The iridescent green backside and wings glistened in the sun as it settled onto a perch. "It reminds me of the dragonflies I see flying over the pond from cattail to cattail." She clicked her tongue. "Even bugs have more favor than I do with color."

A slow creaking sound came from the house as a human tiptoed outside through the back door. It was a young woman. Slow body movements suggested she was mindful of her bird friends at the feeders. The human held something in her hand. With mounting curiosity, Leah studied her as she drew near, one cautious step at a time. Stopping about ten feet from the hummingbird, the human extended her arm out slightly and stood still.

Leah remained, but was ready to take off if the woman moved any closer. She was certain the skittish hummingbird would fly away. Sure enough, it did leave, but, to Leah's amazement, the little bird went straight to the human. Leah stared as the hummingbird whirled around the woman a few times before lowering itself down onto her hand. The bird lighted on a bright flower-type container and began to feed straight from it. It all looked too strange and too dangerous to suit Leah.

"Why isn't that hummingbird afraid? What if it's a nasty trick to catch it? Of course, the human would have to move pretty fast to do that. But, still, anything can happen." Leah held her breath and waited. Finally, the hummingbird left the woman and retreated to the feeder on the pole. The human, apparently satisfied, went back into the house and gently closed the door behind her. "I've just got to ask that hummingbird about this." She flew to the other end of the clothesline and carefully situated herself a few feet away from the hummingbird, who was still keeping a guarded eye on Leah's movements.

"Can I help you with something, Sparrow?"

Leah couldn't tell if the bird was cross or not. It hadn't really reacted to her; at least, not yet. These tiny birds were very territorial and would chase large birds away that dared trespass into their area.

"Hello, Miss Hummingbird. I just watched you do an incredible thing with that human. How could you, why did you do that? I mean, weren't you afraid? Do you always do that? Do all hummingbirds do that? And..."

"Hold it!" blurted out the hummingbird in a small voice. "You sure do have questions, but it'll take me too long to answer them. I have to get back to my little humming-birdies to feed them." Sounding like a bumblebee's drone as her wings flapped, the hummingbird continued, "I'll just say this. I've discovered that I can make humans eat out of my hand."

"What? Wait a minute. *You* were the one eating out of *her* hand."

"Yes, yes, I know. But, it's really how you perceive it. As you can see, the human already puts a feeder out here for me. She's earned my trust, so I have the upper hand. I have her eating out of my hand. Do you understand?"

Leah looked as though she had a huge question mark on her forehead.

The hummingbird sighed. "I didn't just attempt to do this today, little sparrow! This human has been trying to gain my trust for a long time; standing very still, being very quiet, and making sure I always have a feeder full of nectar. So began the trust. Then I saw that it gave her as much pleasure feeding me from her hand as it gave me pleasure satisfying my appetite from it, too."

Leah was deep in thought when the miniature bird continued.

"You see, if the human wanted me close to her, she was the one that had to take the initiative. She proved that she cared for us humming-birds, and her dedication has earned our trust." The hummingbird filled up one last time as she prepared to leave. "There are more of us that come here," she called out to Leah. She was gone in a twinkle of an eye.

"Trust? Who in the world can be trusted?"_

A trill of chirps and clicks distracted Leah. They came from the direction of the regular bird feeders farther into the back yard. Yellow Finches and Chickadees were well filling up on thistle and other seed. A Redheaded Woodpecker made its way to a container of suet; its crimson head bobbing back and forth as its long bill bore into the block.

A sparrow's spring nest was camouflaged by new leaves covering the gray limbs. Tall massive pine trees lined the end of the property with long sweeping arms hanging heavily toward the ground. Leah's eyes fixed onto what she had been looking for—a pair of Cardinals. They had just flown to a nearby honey-suckle vine whose twining limbs were still absent of their sweet flowers. The Cardinal pair chipped to each other their own language, being watchful of what was going on around them. Leah knew them to be a somewhat jittery bird, the slightest sound or movement alternating into hasty flights. She flew to the ground under containers raining down seed from the feeding frenzy of other birds. She decided to wait and see what the Cardinals would do next, hoping they would eventually come to dine close to her. Making their grand entrance, she knew she could hardly miss now. She was within close range of the glorious red feather she wanted, yet no plan as yet to do anything about it.

"The male Cardinal is the one with the brightest feathers compared to his mate. I could rush him, yank off one of them as fast as I can, and make a quick getaway. I'll be out of sight long before he knows what hit him." Leah sighed. "I need a real plan."

Without warning, the male Cardinal ended up right in front of Leah. Embodied in ruby-red brilliance and a pointed crest like no other, Leah could not take her eyes off of him. The color reminded her of the richly colored cherries that grew on a tree at a well-known garden she visited. It was all she could do to keep from blurting out what she desired from the Cardinal right there and then. But, right timing was essential.

"Perfect," Leah breathed out quietly. At least she thought she had.

"What?" the Cardinal asked, looking at her. "Did you say something?"

"Me? Uh, no, sir," she quickly answered, and, as quickly, she chastised herself for not taking the opportunity presented to her. She hoped she hadn't unwittingly missed her chance, because the Cardinal began to distance himself from her.

*Oh, no! What if he's done eating and leaves. I don't always run into Cardinals. I need to make my move now, or it might never come again. I've got to have one of those feathers.*

Leah cautiously made her way toward the Cardinal, hoping to make the bird think she was only after the seed. But, she had a rude awakening. The female Cardinal dive-bombed her, barely missing her head. She ducked, feeling the feathers on her neck rise. Leah had totally forgotten about the female bird. It was a warning. Looking up to check on the attacker, she spotted the female in another tree about a stone's throw away from them. The female Cardinal signaled with hurried clicks to her mate that she was ready to leave. Leah knew she had no time to waste. She edged up closer to the male bird still enjoying his favorite seeds. He stopped in mid-chew and glared at Leah, now clearly aware that she was staring at him. Leah opened her mouth; it was now or never.

"Mr. Cardinal, I don't mean to interrupt your meal, but I've just got to talk to you."

The bemused red bird frowned at her. She was noticeably a strange little bird with two matchless feathers on her wings. At first thought, she could be an Indigo Bunting, a similarly small bird. Female Indigo Buntings are colorless with only a touch of blue on the wings. But, the Cardinal wasn't quite sure after he eyed her long and hard. Leah felt very uncomfortable, fidgeting nervously. He finally spoke up.

"Well, what is it?" he asked. Then, he added with a slight smirk, "What kind of bird are you, by the way?"

"A sparrow, of course," Leah said, rolling her eyes. Although she was embarrassed, defiance broiled inside. She couldn't wait for the time when she would show all her critics who she really was. She would have the last laugh then.

"Huh. Well, I wasn't sure," the Cardinal sniffed. "What you say you are and what you look like are two entirely different things, young lady. What is it you wanted, anyway?" he asked, stealing a glance toward his mate who was still waiting for him. But, he made no move to leave. Novelty seemed to play a big part to stay and find out why a bizarre-looking sparrow would want to talk to him.

"Well, it's that I've always admired your feathers, sir, the bright color, your crested crown, and..."

"Yes, yes! Get on with it."

"What I want to ask, sir, is if I could have one of them?" Leah blurted out fast.

"One of what?"

"One of your red feathers."

"One of my red feathers? What on earth for?" The Cardinal's pointed crest quickly flared up, showing his irritation.

"For a keepsake." That was the only thing that popped into her mind. "Yes, that's why I want it. For a keepsake," Leah reiterated, hoping hard that it would convince him. "You know, like..."

"Like those other feathers you have on your wings already?"

Leah's shoulders drooped. She had not succeeded in hiding her plans from him. All she could do was look down and swish a small pebble back and forth with her foot, unsure of what to do next.

"Aren't those feathers pretty ill-fitting, miss? I dare say it makes flying a bit harder, too, doesn't it? Don't you think adding to them will only aggravate the problem?"

Leah rolled her eyes again and gave a short, quick sigh. *He sounds like my father!* She heard the female cardinal clicking impatiently to her mate. "Yes, sir, it's difficult, but I've been able to manage well enough so far, otherwise I wouldn't be here talking to you right now."

"Well enough, I guess." He gave another look toward his mate and back to Leah. A noticeable nervous slant toward reckless behavior was quite out of the ordinary for a bird as small and meek as a sparrow is usually identified. Yet, the Cardinal sensed a kind of quiet sadness hidden behind the tiny, inquisitive eyes that looked at him as though life itself hinged on what decision he would make. Now it was his turn to roll his eyes and heave a big sigh.

"I suppose a small tuft feather wouldn't hurt," he said, in an aggravated tone. "But, it's against my better judgment." Then, he added more sternly, "It certainly will be enough for you, too, young lady. I will not be held responsible for any accidents or injuries that occur because one of my feathers is attached to you. Do you understand?"

"Yes, sir! Of course not, sir. Thank you so very much, sir!"

Leah's countenance changed like a wind-blown cloud after a rainy day. She waited with bated breath as the Cardinal proceeded to pluck one of his smaller feathers from underneath his wing. He pulled it out and dropped it at her feet. She hurriedly reached for it as the feather began swirling along the ground, being pushed about by a small puff of wind.

"There, I hope you use it wisely." He watched as Leah awkwardly ran after his feather. "But," he said, as he proceeded to look at her other two unmatched feathers, "by the look of things…." The red bird didn't finish his sentence. He flew away to meet his mate who had already flown on ahead of him.

"I don't care what you think," Leah said out loud toward the two silhouettes in the sky. Her chin jutted out. "I know what I'm doing."

She regarded the edge of the backyard that bordered an already cultivated field lined into rows of dark rich soil. The Cardinal couple continued out across the field to a large wood on the opposite side. She was well aware of the crimson color streaking through the air. Now she had her own; she had her crown.

# Chapter 7
## THE CALL

*All wisdom is summed up in two words:*
*Wait and hope.*
*–Alexandre Dumas*

Leah tucked the feather tuft securely between the crisscrossing twigs in her nest so it would not be lifted out by the wind and went in search of the sticky tree glue again. But, looking for the sap was easy compared to her preoccupation over how she would attach the crimson feather on top of her head. She was determined to have it look like the Cardinal's crown. It would be tougher this time around, though. Finding the sap, she headed back to her nest.

A masterful plan was needed. As her thinking process began, she attached the plume to the wall of the nest directly in front of her. Studying the beauty of the color softly painted on the small feather, she could easily picture it on top of her head like a crown.

*Think. Think. I've got to think of a good way to attach this feather, one that will...help me...glue...it.* Leah yawned. She had sat too long already. Looking out onto the pond for the first time since she returned to her nest, she noticed the male Mallard sitting on the smooth water. His pearl-green head shined like an emerald jewel in the rays of sunlight as they cut through the trees. Periodically, the duck would reach under water, its unglamorous bottom and orange feet sticking up, and retrieve savory pond vegetation to eat. One time, as he repeated the action, the duck's supple food landed comically on top of his head as he quickly bobbed back up.

"I know just how I'm going to do it!" Working the feather more securely into the side of the wall, Leah made sure the quill pointed out toward her. She placed a glob of sap onto its tip. Taking a deep breath she bent over and pushed her head forward until she could feel the sharp tip of the quill prick her scalp. "There! I knew I'd come up with a plan to help me attach this feather. All I needed was a little inspiration. Thanks, Mr. Mallard."

But a harsh realization hit her. "How am I going to able to stay in this position until the glue dries?" Leah sighed. "This is going to take forever. If I had thought about it a little bit more, I wouldn't have done it this way." The need to stay still for a long stretch was beyond anything Leah could have imagined. But as she did, an awareness of her surroundings made its way to her ears. Images formed in her mind as she heard particular sounds without the privilege of seeing it with her eyes, as her head was bent downward. Vigorous slapping sounds came from the direction of the pond. "That sound is the duck couple flapping their wings. Probably stretching out." She let out a groan. "How delicious it would feel to do the same thing myself. My poor neck is so stiff already."

It became a game for Leah, a fun distraction. She had seen the ducks demonstrate that sound before; their long necks stretched upwards, beaks pointing toward the ceiling of the woods as they briskly beat their wings back and forth. Leah then heard a steady buzzing trill coming from a tree close to her. Or was it far away? Was it to her right side or to her left? She was aware of the insect's vibrations bouncing off the countless natural barriers in the woods.

"That's a cicada. They sure are a puzzle as to where they really are. It confuses their enemies from finding them, I'm sure. I'm getting good at this game." A repetitive knocking reached her ears. She pictured a Redheaded Woodpecker conducting the beat against a tree trunk.

"That's a Woodpecker. Probably digging holes for a nest or searching for insects. Wait a minute! It could be the clunking sound those annoying little chipmunks make when they talk to each other."

Leah was grateful that she could do something else besides being bored in her nest with a serious pain in her neck and back, but she needed to stretch. The anticipation of it still brought an impatient whimper to her lips. Her self-pity was interrupted by a dog's far away bark. A fainter reply echoed across the great divide of fields and farmyards.

"Those are dogs. Human's pets, loud nuisances, always chasing, always barking."

She heard motorized vehicles on the long expanse of country roads fading into remote places where Leah thought they never returned. The low drone of a tractor's engine sputtered in one of the fields across the many lands far from her woods, accompanied by the melancholy mooing of a lonely cow in a distant meadow. Leah couldn't help but let another yawn escape. "I hear the road machines, the farmer's tractor... those fat cows Mother...used to tell us...about."

The sounds of life streamed into Leah's tired body and mind, causing her to fall sleep. Frogs from the pond serenaded her, adding their rhythmic song of nature. It brought an end to Leah's newfound guessing game. She was now between sleep and wakefulness. Leah heard voices in her spirit like the thuds of a woodpecker—repetitive and bothersome; sounds at the edge of her dream that felt threatening.

A low, ghostly howl floated toward her. Again, the alarming wail came and Leah recognized it was an owl. Even in her oblivion she continued playing guess-the-sound. She pictured the big yellow-eyed owl, its long broad wings full of soft, round-tipped feathers which made them virtually noiseless. Being practically undetected, they were known as attackers in flight, snatching defenseless victims right out of their nests. Someone like her.

Leah couldn't move, couldn't rouse herself. Then a loud clamor shook her to her very core. A band of black crows, crows that were nest raiders, made Leah an easy target where she lay. She struggled to open her eyes, to open to reality, or at least to another dream in which to escape. But, she couldn't shake off the eerie feeling. The struggle to awaken was exhausting her. The battle continued until another sound so uncommon than anything she had heard before shook her out of her prison of dreams.

A loud and fierce piercing cry vibrated around her. She woke up, a frown etched across her face, unsure of what happened. There was a momentary setback as she forgot the reason for her unusual position: her head against the wall of the nest. But, then, another long screech echoed through the atmosphere. In an outburst of wings and loud squawks, the crows high above Leah fled in a hurry and the forest was left quiet and still.

"I remember I was having one of those nightmares again. But, that sound woke me up. What could make a call like that? I've never heard anything so loud. Was it a bird? If it was, it had to be a very big one to make that kind of call."

Yet, it wasn't only the enormous sound that Leah noticed; it was the forcefulness of it that caught her attention. For a reason Leah could not explain, she was not actually frightened by it. Compared to the conflict she had experienced during her nightmarish sleep, the creature's call actually helped her out of it. An explosion of branches breaking and crashing against each other startled her. Straining her neck to search the sky for the cause of the racket, a deluge of twigs, dried leaves, and pine needles fell all around her making it impossible to see clearly. But, for a split second, she did catch sight of an extremely large and darkish figure heading east.

"Oh, no! My Cardinal feather!"

Leah quickly crouched back down into her nest, hoping her sudden outburst hadn't attracted some undesirables like the owl or the crows in her dream. She looked at the spot she had tucked the feather.

"It's gone! What if it isn't on top of my head? I have to go down to the pond to see for myself. But, what if those evil things from my dream are lurking around?" she whispered, dread welling up inside of her. "What if that creature I heard with that massive voice is still here, too?" Then she sighed with relief as she noticed the forest coming back to life again. The usual sounds filled the air with the constant whir of nature's stirrings. Her eyes searched back and forth through the trees. She spotted a squirrel. "There's that noisy mother squirrel chattering about something else." Leah's heart skipped a beat as a sizeable bird maneuvered through the trees and smoothly lowered itself into the shallow end of the pond. "Relax, Leah. It's only a heron."

A white mist engulfed the slender water bird, creating a ghostlike figure with wings. The heron went knee deep into the water and began its statuesque stance. With its long-beaked head bent over the water,

Leah saw it was ready to spear its food. The pond had plenty of small fish and crawdads for the heron's particular taste.

Although herons didn't frequent her pond, on the occasions they did, they quite fascinated her. She studied the tall bird as a silvery vapor rose from the water and surrounded the already gray bird. With a fluid stabbing motion and barely a gurgle from the water's surface, the heron came up with a struggling crawdad in its beak and readily made it its first morsel.

Leah detected a slight movement to her right in the low undergrowth and observed a large family of grouse. The mother bird led a brood of nine chicks huddled close together; their brown and gray markings making them look like a piece of tree bark moving along the ground. She returned her gaze to the heron once again. They ate almost anything that came close to their feeding area; moles, mice, and even undersized birds.

"Those grouse chicks are so small and vulnerable out there if they wander from their mother." Looking below again, Leah was relieved to see the mother grouse was well aware of the enemy's presence. The leggy heron once again harpooned the water, quickly devouring a tiny silver fish. With her mother's instincts aroused, the grouse scooted her brood back into the brush with incredible swiftness, quietly and orderly.

The water-bird was also ready to leave. It opened its long wings and gave a smooth, swift jump out of the water, lifting easily into the air. It rapidly gained altitude and in no time was high above the trees and out of Leah's sight.

"That heron's gone now, and that stranger with the big voice is gone, too. I'm dying to see if my Cardinal tuft is on top of my head."

Leah's enthusiasm couldn't contain her curiosity any longer. She had been bound to her nest for too long; stretching out felt exhilarating to her. She spread her wings up and out before flying down to the pond, making sure her first two feathers were not out of place. Deep desire took over any fear she might have had about predators. She flew to the bank where small rocks and stones made a handy docking area. She slowly stooped to look at herself, still holding on to the fear that all the work and trouble she went through with the tuft could have all been in vain.

As Leah approached the pond, a small frog jumped into the water causing many little ripples. A frown crossed her face knowing she would have to wait a bit longer to see herself. But, gradually the tiny waves did settle down, and a slow ripple of a smile crossed her face. Her crimson crown was in place.

## Chapter 8

# FINDING HOOZER

*It was not foes to conquer, nor sweethearts to be kind,*
*But it was friends to die for that I would seek and find.*
*-A.E.Housman*

L eah was concerned. She had not run into Hoozer in a long time. It was pretty unusual, as they would frequently show up at the same places. They had the same tastes in feast gardens and enjoyed each other's company. Leah sat on a rock hedgerow next to a lonely dirt road where not many traveled but an occasional tractor and farmer.

"Is he that mad at me?"

A cricket answered with a chirrup in close proximity. Leah quickly looked around to see if she could catch a fast meal, but the cricket cowered underneath a pile of long-embedded rocks for cover. She had flown down to investigate some flying grasshoppers she spied on her way to another favorite spot to eat. She hoped she would spy Hoozer, also.

This favored feast-garden rested on a small hill far from the country road, at the end of a long driveway with tall trees bordering either side. Leah felt the expectation that she would find her cousin at this oasis. They often ran into each other here throughout the summer days, both liking the secluded away-from-the-chaos retreat. The low brick building was surrounded by a huge yard, the front side sloping down toward the main road, dotted throughout with flowering bushes, trees and floral gardens.

Today Leah made this special trip hoping to not only find Hoozer, but also to get something off her chest. After much thought and tossing and turning, she admitted she was too hard on him at their last meeting. There was no excuse for how she treated him, no matter how she was feeling.

*Oh, I do hope he's here. I've got to clear things up with him and apologize.* Leah's spirit was boosted immediately as she entered the feeding area. There he was, enjoying a meal, just as she had hoped. His back was toward her; a mischievous grin spread over her face. *As I recall, he has some payback coming. He'll never know what hit him.*

Leah leveled her wings and softly, quietly, descended onto the unsuspecting sparrow. She screeched as loud as she could and deliberately bumped into him as she landed. She knew she scored extra points against her worthy opponent in the scare factor.

"Aaaah!" Hoozer sailed straight up from the ground with a screech, turning around quickly. "What's going on?" He saw a strange little bird with colorful patches on its wings, laughing fiendishly at his momentary lack of poise. Hoozer let out a giant sigh, relieved that it was not an enemy. "Touche', Leah Sparrow!" he exclaimed good-naturedly, straightening up.

"Got you, Hoozer! You deserve it for scaring the living daylights out of me the last time."

"Boy, you don't forget easily, do you? That was a long time ago. In the spring, I think. Wasn't it?"

"Yeah, something like that. Anyway, I didn't come here just to get back at you, although it was perfect timing, I must admit," Leah said, chuckling. She cleared her throat and became more serious. "Hoozer, I came looking for you because I missed you. I haven't seen you for a long time, thinking you were mad at me. I want to apologize for the way I treated you. It was wrong of me."

Just then Leah realized Hoozer had a strange look on his face. He was staring at her, not saying a word. In her longing to see Hoozer, she had totally forgotten that her appearance had taken quite a different turn since they had been together last. *Oh no. What's he thinking?* Dread filled her heart as to where the next words spoken between them would take them.

"Well, all's forgotten, Leah. There's no harm done," Hoozer started cautiously. He chuckled. "You know me. I just let things roll off me like water off a duck's back."

*He sounds a little strained, and he keeps staring at me.* Leah knew her friend's concern for her would not allow him to stay quiet, no matter how great the threat to their friendship. It was for that very reason, their unnatural camaraderie, which Leah believed Hoozer would dare risk everything to bring to light what was on his mind.

"Leah, what is it with those different feathers on your wings...and on your head?" he asked. "And, why?"

Leah hoped she could avoid an argument again between them. It meant she would have to hold angry words from escaping her mouth, words stemming from a defensive mode, although it would be difficult after baring her soul to him in an apology. She certainly didn't want to do that all over again. She chose her words carefully.

"Well, Hoozer, after much consideration about where I wanted my life to go, that I wanted to look as good as any other bird in the world,

I needed to make a few changes. It boils down to why stay dull and drab looking when I can change things for myself?"

"I never thought you wanted to be anybody else but you, Leah. Why would you want to change the Leah I know that's easy to get along with, kind to others, and adventurous? I don't understand."

"I know you don't understand, Hoozer. You don't have to understand. Nobody has to but me, because it's about *me*."

"But, I want to understand. Help me a little here. Why do you think you need this kind of altering from the real sparrow you are?" Hoozer paused. "Hey, wait a minute. Is that what was bothering you in the spring when you got mad at me back then? You were feeling bad about yourself, weren't you? I remember you were looking into the water-mirror when I came up behind you. You were acting pretty weird."

"You know, Hoozer, I came to find you because I missed you and all you're doing is analyzing me." Angry, Leah readied herself to fly away.

"Leah, wait! Please, wait. I'm sorry. I didn't mean to make you angry. I tried hard not to. I just want to know what's going on with my friend. That's all. I really do want to support you, Leah. I'm trying to understand. Really I am."

Resentment began to evaporate as she saw a deep concern etched on Hoozer's face. She exhaled a long drawn-out breath, her cheeks ballooning as the air escaped her tight lips. It was time for apologies again.

"Ok. I'm sorry, too, Hoozer. Again. I've become so defensive whenever anyone questions me about what I'm doing. I get fuming mad and it rises up in me faster than lightening going across the sky."

"Tell me about it," Hoozer chuckled.

Leah let out a soft laugh, too. "I guess I just have to accept the fact that no one will probably understand, but ultimately it's just me that's got to feel good about it. You know, feel good about *me*."

"Well, as far as I'm concerned, Leah, I like you the way you are. I'm here for you all the way. I'll cover your back, and you cover mine. Agreed?"

"Agreed," Leah echoed. She responded with more joy than she had felt in a while. That's why she loved being around this fine House Sparrow cousin of hers. He could always say the right things at the right time to settle her heart. "Let's enjoy the fine food here, and then we can go get a cool drink at that child-statue with the upside down umbrella. Water is always in it."

"Sounds good to me," Hoozer said. "I think I'm going to stay in this area for awhile just to get this special seed the humans put out. Are you?"

"I don't think so." Leah was anxious to continue her search for more feathers, but she couldn't let Hoozer know. Even after their heart-to-heart talk, Leah sensed he hadn't really accepted all she shared. But, spending time with him was always a special treat.

As the afternoon sun lazed its way down behind the house, the two found themselves perched in a perfume-infused flowering bush. The bronze statue with an inverted umbrella was filled with water and stood only a few yards away. Hanging feeders swung lightly only a short way in the opposite direction. The two comrades were full, happy, and resting as the day settled into its conclusion.

Leah looked up to the sky. Soon it would be sparkling with the crystals of heaven. She began to feel sentimental for the long ago days when she and her siblings were cozily crowded in their nest. It was almost a blur to her now, like the stars above her not yet fully exposed. Suddenly, she felt like telling a story, her ancestor's story, the one her father shared with her family. Since she had a captive audience of one, she turned to Hoozer.

"Hoozer, do you want to hear a great story?"

"Well, do I have a choice?"

"No, you don't. Ha-ha!"

"Well, then, storyteller, share away."

Leah beamed at what Hoozer called her. That's what she had admired about her father. He was a great storyteller, one whose narratives pierced her heart as she felt connection to her long ago forebears.

"Thanks, Hoozer. I'll tell you the great legend of my ancestral Chipping Sparrow origins. My father told it to my siblings and me when we were just tiny birdies. But, this part is after the original two Chipping Sparrows- Spayro and Chippy- met way up there in the great vast universe." Leah looked up longingly, searching for the stars in the graying dusk. She remembered her father doing the same thing as he shared their life story, with countless white diamonds shining down on them as witnesses.

"Well, now I'm real curious."

"Good. Here goes. Uh-hum." Leah cleared her throat. "A caeli enarrari- the heavens declare," she whispered mysteriously. "Spayro and Chippy were now one. When they met, the impact was so great that it caused an explosion of like-onto-like forms, millions of them gushing forth from Spayro and Chippy. They were indeed made for each other.

"We can't stay here forever, Chippy. We need to populate some other fine place."

"I agree, Spayro. We need to move forward to find the best place they can grow up."

"I think it's time to go see the Great Spirit Luz. He'll advise us on the best thing to do."

The new parents approached the grand city where Luz lived. It could not be missed; it lit up the whole eastern space of the universe. Spayro and Chippy were ushered into his presence immediately.

"Welcome, Spayro! Welcome, Chippy! How are you both doing today? I hear you are proud parents of millions of babes. Wonderful! What can I do for you on this fine universe-day?"

"Thank you, Great Spirit Luz," Spayro said. "We are doing just fine. We come today seeking your favor and advice for us and our babes."

"Certainly. My favor and advice is always yours," he boomed, laughing. Always enthusiastic about good things happening throughout the cosmos, he bid Spayro to continue. "What is it you are seeking, Spayro? I dare say you want to travel far away with Chippy and that entire brood of yours. Right?"

"Yes, sir, we do." His eyebrows raised in surprise at how Luz already knew their plans. "We feel we can accomplish much more somewhere else. Our babes can then find new places of their own. They could spread out all over to populate it and bring happiness to other lands from our species. That's my heart's desire."

"Wonderful idea, Spayro. I know just the place for you to go and keep multiplying. There is a certain species called Humans that I'm sure you will enjoy, on a planet called Earth."

"Earth. Hmm. It sounds like a good name."

"It is a very good name. It's covered with grand mountains, lush valleys, green meadows, tall trees, and beautiful plants. It's got many different waters: deep, wide oceans, beautiful clear lakes, and lovely winding rivers. There are hot deserts, cold snow-lands, and lovely islands. There are wonderful things to see, to eat, and to do. "

"I believe we want to go to Earth, sir. Right, Chippy?"

"Indeed we do, sir. It sounds like the perfect place we would all love."

With a big smile, Spayro nodded his head in approval. "If it's alright with you, sir, we will go now."

The Great Luz gave a hearty laugh. "That's enthusiasm for you. Now, I give to you my favor and my blessing that you go and multiply your species and your clan on Earth, beginning today. From this day forth, you will be known as the Chipping Sparrows."

"Thank you, Great Spirit Luz. We will certainly do as you say."

Their leader paused for a second before dismissing the couple. His face held both a slight concerned, yet inquisitive, look at the same time.

"I want to ask a favor of you, Spayro, my friend."

"Certainly, sir. I will try my best to do what you desire."

"I would like to ask if you and Chippy would kindly leave a few of your babes here with me to make their nests by my throne. They are one of a kind, you know, very special to me. They can join my swallows here, too. It just makes my heart soar watching them."

Spayro and Chippy looked at each other and smiled.

"Of course, Great Luz. A group of our Chippies has already asked our permission to stay in the universe with you. We know they will bring you much joy. They did to us."

"Wonderful! I thank both of you very much. I wish you all the best on Earth."

"Good-bye, Great Spirit Luz."

Spayro and Chippy exited the radiant place with its many rainbow rays illuminating the path in front of them. The enormous Chipping Sparrow family was directed to what looked like a doorway on the floor of the universe; a door between Luz' domain and Earth. The parents looked through it together.

"What a beautiful looking sphere, Spayro!"

"Yes, it is. Well, here we go, my love. It looks like it's going to be a wild ride."

"I trust you'll get us all down there safely, and together we'll find the best place as our home."

"Agreed."

Spayro looked back at his large brood, and before giving the signal to take that first plunge, he spoke. "My family, as we go through open space, we will feel a Voice in our spirits. It will reveal to us our purpose as Chipping Sparrows, our new name for our species on the planet called Earth. We will hear where the best places are for us to live, how to make nests, and what to use to build them. We will hear what we can eat and what we can drink; we will know whom we can trust and whom to stay away from. So listen carefully. Our lives depend on it. But, remember, we will fill the hearts of the Humans with happiness."

With one great voice, they responded, "Yes, father!"

As Spayro flew through the opening, he yelled, "Free-fall to Earth!"

"Free-fall to Earth!" the rest of the clan echoed. Immediately, a unique understanding flooded their spirits in unison. They were embarking on a special route to Earth. Instantly, they began to feel a gentle, yet firm, voice speaking to them just as their father had told them. As they approached Earth's atmosphere, they began transforming into a different form. Their light-form covered up in soft sleek growths called feathers. Parts of these feathers grew outward and longer on either side of their bodies, creating a wind barrier that lifted them up in the air as they hit Earth's skyway. These were called wings. Their new wings gave them much freedom as they flew toward new territories far and wide, a place to call their home.

At the end of instruction, the Voice stopped. They had reached Earth, and each had dispersed to their intended destination. Spayro and Chippy found their own place, too. Theirs was a great beginning on Earth and were very happy to the very end, multiplying many new birdies. This is the legend of our clan, 'Spizella Pesserina', the Chipping Sparrows. The End."

"That was awesome, Leah. It's great that your family clan has a story that can be told over and over to each generation. It helps you know who you…uh, who you…." Hoozer's voice trailed off. He turned his head as he pretended to look around for something, avoiding eye contact with Leah.

"Hoozer, I know you were going to say something else," she said. "Come on, out with it." Hoozer continued looking around. "I won't get mad. Well…I'll try not to get mad. At least you'll have your say. Now, tell me."

Hoozer's shoulders hung down a little. "Alright, Leah, but remember, you told me to tell you. It's just that I don't understand… there's that word again. I *want* to understand why it was so important for you to share your clan's story about how they came to be, how they came to Earth, their name and all, but you have no desire to *be* like them." Hoozer waited with bated breath. "There, I said it."

"It's not the same, Hoozer," Leah exclaimed. She knew another big gap could come between them if she didn't exhibit control more prominently than her new feathers. "I love the story, I love my ancestors. I just don't want to look like them. I want more color. I want to sing better. That's all. Colors like the Blue Jays, a crown like the Cardinal's. I want to sing like the Yellow Warbler, to be known for my songs. What's wrong with that?"

"Leah, a family is made up of those you come from, and so, in turn, your inheritance. You have no choice whatsoever how you come out. That's nature. One just has to accept it, or…" Hoozer hesitated a second time.

"Or what?

"Or you end up being pretty miserable about yourself."

"What makes you think I'm miserable?"

"Forget it, Leah. I've already said too much. I'm just worried about you and don't want anything bad to happen to you. That's all. I just want to help you in any way I can."

"You don't have to worry about me, Hoozer. I'm doing just fine. I don't need your help, or anybody else's, for that matter. I can take care of things myself, just like I did getting these feathers. All… by…myself." Leah quickly left the branch and flew in the direction of her home.

"Leah! Wait! I was only trying to help!" But, the sincere pleading fell on deaf ears. Hoozer could only stare. His perch swung as he gazed at Leah's tiny form fading into the dusk.

"Oh, Leah," he whispered. Now he was scared for her. He knew no amount of persuading was going to change her mind. He saw she was dead set in her ways. "I sure hope she makes it home safe."

Leah knew it was a matter of time before the graying evening would settle into nighttime. Once again she let her anger get the better of her, and once again she directed it at her dear friend. He always had good things to say to her and never tried to hurt her intentionally.

"Well, that meeting went well. Now I don't even know if we'll ever see each other again."

Leah's tears almost blinded her as she entered her woods. Her heart was hurting, not only because of the fear of losing a friend, but because of the truth that resounded in her ears.

# Chapter 9
## SHADOW

*Yet is every man his greatest enemy,*
*And, as it were, his own executioner.*
*- Sir Thomas Browne*

Leah spent the better part of the day searching for favorite foods. Caterpillars and grasshoppers were abundant in the midst of June's stifling temperatures. Earth had set its natural course in bringing forth its full mantle of flowers. Mother Nature was also raising its young. Leah's daily flights took her to area farms where the newest additions to the animal kingdom made life a little bit noisier. Yellow, fluffy chicks scurried around their mother's legs, learning to scratch and scrape for their food. It was the fine intricacies of life lessons: little eyes watching the bigger, trusted look-alike in front of them to imitate important survival skills. Curious calves looked at the New World through large doe-like eyes, though not straying far from their mother's presence and warm milk.

But, the loss of sensitivity to the newborns around Leah went unnoticed, for the most part. Sitting on the top rung of a wooden fence that encircled a small herd of horses, she felt troubled. The huge farm was half way between Leah's nest home and the Big Waters—a vast body of bluest water. She didn't always travel this far. There was plenty of food where she lived, but without really knowing why, she found herself in faraway places at times. Distant bells tolled clearly from a small town where humans lived close to the Big Waters. The continual winds rolled into the sound of the bells, carrying them farther inland. Leah had for the first time smelled the ocean air with its perfect suggestion of water and sand and fish.

But, her spirit was closed to all of the poetic existence of the day. She was waiting. Waiting for glimpses of a beetle or two crawling on the tall grasses growing along the rails; waiting for a caterpillar moving slowly along the fence. She wasn't very hungry, but she knew she had to eat. Eating was only a necessity anymore to Leah, something she endured just to stay alive, and this was one of those times. As the persistent need for new feathers grew, her daily need of even the most common needs was challenged. She found it hard to concentrate on anything else.

Something in the corral distracted her from further search of a meal. The pasture held a special group of horses; they were mothers, each with a new colt of their own. Many of the youngsters were asleep on the ground close by their mother's protective hulk, the edges of their big shadows barely inches from their colts. Although most of the young ones were asleep under the alluring sun, Leah heard a high-pitched whinny coming from among them.

Searching the group, she spotted a light-tan colt with long unsteady legs; it was only a few weeks old and the only one awake. It was standing in front of its Palomino mother, but he didn't stay there for long. He began running about in short spurts, bucking his hind legs as though striking at some unseen foe. Even his wobbly stance did little to deter him from showing persistence in discovering just how much he could do. Throwing his head up and down and shaking it with passion, it let out some rousing whinnies.

*He's an excited little thing. I think he's trying to impress his mother.* Leah was now very curious about the four-legged animal.

After the fuss was over, the colt stood right in front of his mother again in an uncertain stance, as though challenging his parent to a fun joust. Leah saw the mother reach for her babe with a playful nudge, making sweeping shakes of her massive head, and let out a playful snort. The little horse began his charade once again. Once more the breathless colt stood in front of his mother, although this time allowing her to nuzzle him. He, in turn, teasingly nibbled her neck. They exchanged soft murmuring sounds. Leah could almost feel the little colt's vitality, the joy, the total abandon, spiriting toward her. It was the flawless innocence of new life emanating from him that began to ride the wind into her weakened, haggard one.

Leah watched as the colt settled down and began to nurse. She heard the low, throaty murmuring from the mother as she turned her head to look at her exhausted and hungry colt. The smaller horse then sprawled out onto the warm ground next to its mother. Sleep became its master. The mother Palomino took dutiful position as guard over her little one.

An odd thing began to happen to Leah. She suddenly became aware of the aesthetic mood cast by her surroundings. Bees crisscrossed the air with their buzzing strain, searching the open meadows sprinkled with pink mallows and the round, delicate Queen Anne's lace. In their secretive way, they followed the invisible trail back to the nest where their own queen awaited the worker's find.

Leah picked up the chirruping of a cricket nearby, singing its lone tale to no one in particular. The shiny black body snuggled just inside a wide crack in the post. Its long, thin antennae stuck out of the cubbyhole, flicking at every chirrup beat. But, Leah wasn't interested in cricket food at the moment (a lucky thing for the insect, as crickets were one of her favorite foods). For the first time since she returned from her winter home, she was more interested in what was going on around her.

Looking back to the colt still sleeping on the ground, Leah meditated on the great fervor he showed in his few short days of life, more so than she had lived in hers so far. But she smiled. Joy crept into her heart as she reviewed what she had seen in the little one. What made his new life so different from her young life? What made her fear what was deemed her? The little horse showed anything but fear.

Yet, close behind the fresh thoughts barged the unforgotten whispers here, the few questions there, the deliberate jabs other times, and the confusion of life's unfairness barreled into her as she scrutinized once again her life as a sparrow-bird. A frown quickly diffused any joy that had covered her heart just a few moments before.

"That's the problem," she muttered. "I don't have a life to rouse about like that colt. That's why I need these feathers, and more of them. How can anyone like the way I look? *I* don't like the way I look." Like a sudden rain cloud bursting over a picnic, a downpour of despair came over her once again. She was shielded from receiving any more freedom the colt had unknowingly empowered toward her. "What's the use? The colt has someone to watch over him. I'm all alone." Losing the fight over misery, Leah forgot about her one true friend that sincerely wanted peace for her even more than she did.

A small, gust of wind suddenly blew from behind and unsettled some of her feathers. Leah cranked her neck back to tuck them back into place. She froze. Crouched low and menacingly, ready to pounce, with glassy eyes terribly fixed on Leah, was a black cat. Its legs pumped rhythmically underneath its body, anticipating that grand bounding act that is customarily and skillfully executed by all cats on the prowl for prey.

*Shadow!* Everything inside of Leah screamed in terror.

She was doomed. There was no chance for escape. Leah was well aware that cats could jump to tremendous heights when it came to getting what they wanted. Even if she flew upwards, to the left or to the right, the cat's prowess could reach up in the momentum of its leap with no difficulty and snatch her right out of the air with its sharp killer claws. And, indeed, the cat did jump. It sprang up toward her like a shot from a sling. There was only a heartbeat left between her and death.

Leah did the unexpected. She felt an overwhelming urge to drop to the ground in a free fall to thwart the devil cat's design on her. In that split second before the cat could jump over the fence and onto the ground after her, she would quickly fly away to safety. Knowing the cat's extraordinary ability to recover fast, she knew that a split second was all that was allotted her in this fight for life.

She dropped down off the fence. Spreading her wings for balance, Leah suddenly felt a heavy thud on her back. It was the cat's paw crashing on top of her, propelling her down even faster. The feline's claws couldn't dig into her flesh because of her downward direction. She had escaped the first part of the battle, but she had to win this war. Leah desperately needed another split-second window to escape in one piece once she hit the ground.

But, as she approached the last space before crashing, she heard the most fearsome screech right behind her. It came from the cat. Though in a frenzied rush to flee death, Leah wondered what could have made the feline cry out so horrendously as though it was in great pain. She didn't have time for any more thoughts because even more startling was what she heard after Shadow's bellow.

A tremendous shriek of ear-splitting proportions rang out so brutally that Leah was sure it was heard all around the world. What startled her more was the fact that she had heard this sound before. She was sure of it; the same one she heard back in her woods not too long ago. It was that same alarming, yet mesmerizing voice from the strange beast that silenced everything else around the woods; the voice that had awakened her out of the dizzying dream.

Leah collided with the ground harder than she had calculated. It took her breath away. The pounding of horse's hooves could be heard as the ground shook violently under them. Leah felt the vibrations shake her body. The horses had retreated to the far end of the pasture As quickly as she could, she gathered herself up to fly, but she found she was encased in the thick overgrown weeds growing freely along the fence. It was like a cage; the tall, dry, sturdy stems were strong and dense. Trapped in its thickness, Leah felt she lost that window of flight she had hoped for. It seemed to her that the cat was ahead of the game now. He surely had ample time to pounce on her and take her out because he was right behind her. All she could do was brace for the end; she huddled over and closed her eyes.

*I'm a wide-open target for Shadow now!* Shivering like a leaf, her wings over her head, she again waited for the inevitable. Yet, instead of the full weight of an angry cat and its hot breath of death on her neck, instead of the sharp teeth clamping down into her body, instead of the pain and a quick dark end, Leah felt nothing. She heard nothing, and she saw nothing.

*Where is he? Is he waiting for me to make a first move so he can have the game of chase or something?*

Leah heard about cats and their tactics from her parents. They were notorious players, great teasers with their sorry prey. Known to kill without even the need for sustenance, they would toy with their victims before their wretched end. Horror stories traveled the bird-vine telling of feline terrors killing mice, chipmunks, and other unfortunates. Afterwards, they would deliver the dead carcasses to their human master's doorsteps. What the humans would do with the bodies afterwards was beyond anything Leah could even imagine. To her, cats were the worst of the bird kingdom enemies.

She heard a rustle of grass a few feet to her right. Carefully she lifted her head to look. It was Shadow! But, he wasn't coming to attack her. In fact, he wasn't even facing her. He was in a half-seated position on the ground, his back toward her. Leah was more curious about what she saw of the dreadful cat and the absence of an assault than grasping that a great window of opportunity had opened wide for her. Stupefied, she watched from behind the grasses that had slightly straightened up around her. Shadow was shaking his head vigorously. He slowly got up on all fours and swayed back and forth unsteadily.

Leah knew she was risking everything by hanging around this dangerous place. Even though Shadow seemed to falter, she knew all too well that it could turn around quite swiftly. But, as soon as she prepared to leave, carefully guarding her moves to not attract the cat's attention, another daunting screech broke out through the air, sending a jolt of electricity through her body. This time it zapped every last bit of strength she had.

The cat wailed piteously a second time in Leah's short encounter with him, and she saw him retreat toward the barn at breakneck speed. Weaving in and out of the grasses along the fence, it was as though Shadow was fleeing his own mortal enemy—a dog.

Leah didn't know whether to breathe a sigh of relief that Shadow was gone, or if she should brace for a second round of this death battle. Any elation from surviving Shadow could be short-lived. She knew something big made the second horrific sound and it was very close. She sensed its presence like a cold winter breeze on her neck, her skin prickly from fear. What kind of creature could she be dealing with now? Was it another bird-eating enemy? To her amazement, something in her compelled her to turn around for a look.

Nothing could have prepared her for what she saw. Casting a huge shadow over her little body was the most gigantic bird Leah had ever seen. With immense wings spread out from its side, it blocked the bright afternoon light like an eclipse. Around its enormous body a golden sheen outlined its head down to the tips of its great wings as though an electric current emanated from it. Leah jerked her head back down from shock. It was all she could tell of the thing: huge, dark, and nightmarish. Hawks that have ventured close to her territory, she can remember their size, but this one was nothing compared to a hawk. This one was a monster.

The whole terrible ordeal with Shadow and this strange beast above her took only a few minutes, though to Leah it was a lifetime. She decided to look up onto the rail where just minutes before she had been observing the colt, where Shadow had hurled himself at her, and where now the strange beast stood. To her utter dismay, the creature's massive head was bent down toward her, only a few life-saving feet away. That was enough. Without further hesitation, Leah thrust through the heavy foliage as fast as she could and flew away with all the strength she could marshal. She flew the opposite direction Shadow had run, sparing her yet another perilous situation as she flew away from a worse one. Unnerving realization came to her that when she stayed on the ground for extended periods of time too many confusing and dangerous things conspired against her. Although a bird's place wasn't only in the air or in the trees high above, it was also on the ground where evil lurked about.

*That thing could be following me! I'll fly low to the ground. At least I can make it harder for it. With wings that big it'd need to expand to its fullest capacity to have the power to fly. With wings that big it could easily crash into these trees standing too close together.*

Leah escaped into the woods hoping the monster couldn't follow her where she was going. With faltering strength at every beat of her wings, she concentrated heavily on the safety awaiting at her nest home. That was her driving force, though the new feathers felt like lead weights to her. She couldn't understand. She was meticulous about grooming them down so as not to interfere with flying. She landed on a thick-foliage pine to catch her breath. Her nest was four long fields away, far for any small bird with a frightened heart. After a quick break, she headed southward hoping to avert the huge bird from following her. It didn't need to know where she lived, though it took her by a longer route and she was terribly tired.

It was a tight patch of woods she came to rest in this time, very dense and protective. Leah went deeper through the trees until she felt secure that the closed-in area would be detrimental to the huge bulk of feathers she believed was following her. Her heart was pounding in her ears and breath came in short, quick spurts. She stopped and backed into the corner of a branch meeting the thick trunk of a tree. Leah leaned into it for support. She listened for signs of danger, peering through the clutter of branches and pine needles. Nothing seemed out of the ordinary. As her breathing settled to a slower beat, a tiny sliver of hope entered her heart that the dark menace had given up on her.

"If that thing had been after me he would have overtaken me a long time ago," she whispered. She continued looking all around just to make sure. Then, another thought occurred to her. "But what if that thing is waiting for me just outside the woods here? It could be in the next patch of trees, or it could even be hovering in the sky waiting for me to come out." Her mind raced with plans for the next move to gain closer access to her nest without running into the enemy.

Occasionally, a normal-sized bird would fly by. It half-tempted her to join them, hoping that two were better than one to ward off the large intruder. Without a doubt, she would have heard about this stranger from other birds, or she would have seen it long before now. No one could miss a giant like that and not tell about it.

"If that thing was out there, wouldn't it have gone after others like me, too? For that matter, why would it want such a small bird like me? I couldn't possibly be enough for a meal. That devil cat Shadow was more its size."

With her thoughts racing, Leah realized that, in fact, the giant bird didn't go after Shadow, either, though it had the excellent opportunity to overcome him and kill him. Waiting in the trees, Leah hadn't seen any evidence that other creatures and birds were hurrying for shelter from a fierce ravager of small animals. The forest was just as noisy and full of activity as any woods. But, she still found it hard to move out from her hiding place, not convinced that she was safe yet.

Then a familiar sound filtered through the woods as the breeze picked up more movement from the east. As she listened, the steady tempo jogged her memory to where she had heard the sound before. It was the music of the tolling bells that was traveling the wide-open area, being carried on the warm current of air toward her from the white-steeple church by the Big Waters. The once intense sun mellowed to a glow of crimson-pink and orange, firing up the sky. The soft song of the bells floated their light strains around her, filling her with calm. Then Leah caught something through a bare area in the tree's branches that led to an open meadow. It was a field no longer in use and nature had taken over, dressing it in a sea of wildflowers and weeds. Without thinking, she flew off her tree of safety and went to another spot at the edge of the woods for a better look.

In the lowering sun's bright yet soft glow, she saw hundreds of tiny white filaments from the matured dandelions drifting in the air, appearing to dance to the bell song. She watched with growing delight as the sun anointed them with its shimmering light. Soon, tiny insects sailed about like wisps of dust. In this world of glowing iridescence, something once again pierced Leah's spirit just like it had when she watched the young colt. The dandelion heads, the insects, also, were fulfilling their call to freedom over flowers, grasses, land and waters; wherever the miniscule entities desired to light upon.

A smile slowly formed on Leah's tired face. "That's a peaceful sound, in a way like the old human that coos to us birds. Hearing the bells, seeing this nice scene, watching the sun go down..." Leah stopped. "The sun's almost down! I've got to get out of here. I hope that monster has gone far away from here...from me." She flew out of the woods toward her nest home. "The only conclusion I have is that a bird that size has to live far away, somewhere where it can't be seen too easily. It must have flown home before the sun went down. Most birds aren't nocturnal. I sure hope this one isn't either."

# Chapter 10

# THE SEAGULL

Leah sat wide-awake, thrilled with the sight at the pond. The Mallard ducks were now proud parents of eight tiny ducklings full of yellow softness and energy. Already paddling behind their mother, like wind-up toys, their noisy clamor allowed others to be aware of their presence. Fresh with innocence, they were a little tribe of excitement.

High, pristine, white clouds ballooned above as patches of cerulean winked through the changing formations. Very early, the little brood went in the water to swim, flowing into it with ease. Less than a day old and they were already excellent swimmers. Leah watched them with growing curiosity.

"Water is their source of life for food and for protection against enemies. Then they'll learn to fly. It's just like trees are for me, or like being up in the air. I hope they accept their call in life because it'll keep them safe." She stopped and let out a sigh of exasperation. "You hypocrite! You seem to have had a few close calls for not keeping safe yourself. I better take my own advice." Leah chided herself with no mercy. "The ducklings are only just learning about life, fresh out of their eggs, and out into an unknown world. But, I, on the other hand, have been around for a while. No excuses left to allow life catch me off guard."

Leah watched the mother duck climb onto the bank with all her little ones scrambling up behind her. But the last duckling had trouble mastering the higher level. It slipped on the wet grass along the edge a few times, sliding right back into the water.

"I bet he's the runt of the family." She had tender feelings about runts; always the last one, many feelings of neglect, always being compared. At one point the little duck did a clumsy back flip and went totally under. He shot right back up with peeps of terror. The adult Mallard lowered her head down to him with soft raspy sounds of encouragement. Finally, to Leah's delight, the tiny waterfowl conquered its mountain and joined the others. The duckling trundled off and began feeding alongside his siblings.

"Now there was something the little runt learned today: never give up. He kept trying even when it looked impossible for him, even though he was afraid. He'll be a champion someday."

The frightful creature from days ago loomed into her mind. Though its huge, ominous figure overwhelmed her with doom, Leah remembered something else. For the split second she had looked up, an incredible thing happened between them. Leah sucked in a quick intake of breath: their eyes had met. It had been completely blocked from her mind by fear. Yet there was something sneaking into her spirit that was even more piercing than the fear she had felt, more profound than the considerable hulk that had stood above her with, what now seemed to her, no evil toward her.

"What is it?" She dug deep inside to find the answer. Then, slowly, like the opening of the sun at the crack of dawn, the answer came. "It was what I saw in its eyes."

They were huge, round, golden-brown globes, topped by deep furrowed brows. Eyes that penetrated her own, eyes like none she had seen before. They were not the look of a hungry hunter searching for prey, nor were they daggers of death piercing her soul like Shadow's eyes were only seconds before he was stopped in his tracks.

"I was a sitting duck down there on the ground, quick and easy fodder for that huge thing. It could have easily taken that devil cat out for a meal, too. But, it didn't. Shadow lives, and so do I. It's almost like...like it wanted to save..." Leah stopped. "No-o-o. That's ridiculous!" She was shocked where her thoughts were taking her.

A commotion at the pond interrupted her reflections. It was father Mallard. He entered the woods and skillfully landed on the water, arousing his mate who cackled a loud welcome. The commotion stirred up the tinier Mallards who joined the festivities with a gushing chorus. A low drone overhead made Leah look up through the opening above the pond. It was an airplane, and it glinted in the morning sun like shining silver.

"Huh. That flying machine reminds me of the way a seagull shines so silvery in the sky." She watched its westward flight as it slowly disappeared. Then a shine of another kind burst into her senses. "A seagull feather! That's the next plume in my collection."

Immediately, any sleep remaining in her eyes, any questions about her confusing encounter with the feathered giant, any fearful memory of Shadow's leap of death, all disappeared like a popped balloon. Leah was eagerly entertaining a new plan to find a new feather.

"I need to head to the Big Waters. That's where they fly. It'll be a long flight, but I can do it." A cold shiver went through her. "But what if that monster thing is out there by the Big Waters? What'll I do then?"

But panic lingered only a few seconds. Another new feather outweighed the fear of encountering any adversity along the way. Leah readied herself to fly out of her nest. She flapped her wings, straightened any wayward feathers, and checked that the new ones were intact.

The Mallard family was in the pond. The father went upside-down into the water fishing for watery vegetation. Coming up with dark greenery hanging from his beak, the little ones attacked. Leah noticed a couple of stronger and faster ducklings won out over the others, in particular, the runty one that had trouble with the high bank. She sighed.

"It always seems that way. The smaller ones always get left out." Survival of the strongest was the way of life in the animal kingdom; Leah knew that. One learns to live and to stay alive by battling whatever is necessary to extend that life. "That little one will have a big battle ahead of him to survive," she said, watching with sadness. "I sure hope he makes it."

She hopped out to the end of the limb. Opening her wings she flew off the branch toward the rising sun, the blanket of dawn covering her. Covering her, too, were the thoughts of her own survival. Securing new feathers was like engaging in a battle. She hadn't figured the need to take such extreme measures as she's undergone. But, to her there was no other recourse to look beautiful or to feel confident. Now she was getting a new addition toward that end—a seagull feather.

After some stops to feed and rest, Leah found herself close to the horse farm where the near-death experience with Shadow and the monster bird happened. She admitted she had not been alert to what was going on around her, which nearly cost her life. Lately she'd been too distracted, and that was not good for a bird. But, she remembered the moments of the colt and its energetic spirit floating to her, a timely meeting of the two; one with the compulsion of exhibiting it profusely, the other one in need of receiving it.

Making a wide detour south of the farm, she paid closer attention to everything around her. Flying low past another farmhouse farther down the road, Leah saw a curious sight; a family of kittens running and jumping as they chased each other in a sunny spot of the yard. Leah saw how they were being prepared for life as predators. The world had just become more dangerous.

*Watch out, bird-world, they'll be big dangerous hunters soon.*

A puzzling thought had Leah wondering whether cats traveled far from their own habitat in search of prey, because she was thoroughly confused seeing Shadow at the horse farm. He lived at least four fields west of there. It was as though he actually had nine lives, as the word goes about them. Or did all cats just look alike? All her sparrow clan looked alike, as did all other sparrow clans of their own kind. One thing she was positive about was that Shadow was a devil-cat, as she believed all cats were. She could safely say that he wouldn't be traveling to that farm any time soon. She chuckled as she pictured for the hundredth time the shocked tomcat furiously scrambling away.

Several birds entering and exiting a tree-filled yard meant there was food. She flew down onto the low branches of a dogwood tree. Busy Chickadees, Cardinals, different clans of sparrows and a few Yellow Finches made up most of the feeding group. A woodpecker made his entrance onto the trunk of a tree and pecked at some delicacy hidden in its crevices, the back of its head standing out like a bright red apple.

A chipmunk, ever-present at seed gardens, was standing upright, its paws holding seeds to its constant chomping mouth.

Flying down, Leah landed by some distant cousins and began enjoying her favorite seed scattered lavishly on the ground. She was particularly fond of canary seed, finding it only on rare occasions, and only when the Humankind had house birds confined in their homes. Remembering a particular feast garden from the previous summer, she had fed close to a window and heard a bird singing a different type of song. Flying to a higher level, she saw a diminutive bird through a window, yellow and light-blue in color, with a rather short beak, singing from behind some wires of a cage.

Leah noted that this bird was unable to fly, at least not very far. From the water bowl to a swinging perch to its food cache, back and forth, over and over again the little bird flew. This shocked her. She couldn't understand how a caged bird would want to sing under such confined conditions. It wasn't able to live the way it was meant to live, flying without restraint, singing freely in the great outdoors, and eating amply from earth's abundant table. To Leah that bird was a prisoner. She felt sorry for it back then and wondered if the little bird even had a clue of its sorry plight. At one point, the house bird stopped singing and for a few seconds their eyes connected. But, shortly, it continued its high-pitched cantata, habitually flying its short route in the cage. It was a disturbing sight that stayed with Leah for a long time.

Now, a year later, as she ate canary seed at another garden, she was in no mood to find out if there was another captive bird in this house. She held the good thoughts about finding a seagull feather to add to her collection. Eating now was only to gain enough strength for the long flight still ahead to the Big Waters.

Leah felt a sensation creeping all over her flesh, aware that many eyes were staring at her. She still had not grown accustomed to it. In her travels far and wide in search for food, many birds gawked at her as though their eyes were betraying them. She had decided it was easier to ignore them then to get angry.

*If they don't have the common courtesy to say what's on their minds, then I won't give them the satisfaction of knowing anything about me. I've come too far to abandon my dream.*

Suddenly, a light whistling sound landed close to her. Leah looked up to see a Mourning Dove settle and begin to eat. She stole quick peeks at the female dove and she began comparing herself to this total stranger. The dove was over twice as long as Leah, down to its long, tapered tail. She had a soft whisper of gray color with a hint of pink-ish-wash underneath; her wings lightly specked with a bluish cast to them. A fine white line encircled small, black dots for eyes.

*Yeah, she's gray, but her colors are far softer and prettier than mine are. I'd take those grays instead of my dull ones any time. I would have liked a long sleek tail like hers, too.* Leah quarreled with her-self as she added up her miserable comparisons. *I wish I had her long smooth feathers, too.* She paused. *Hm-m. If I had everything I just said I wanted, I would be a dove!* She chuckled out loud.

The dove looked up and smiled. "What's so funny?"

"I'm sorry. I was just thinking about something, that's all. I didn't mean to disturb you."

"No problem," the dove cooed politely. She continued looking at Leah for a few seconds. "Can I ask you a question?"

*Here it comes. I got what I was complaining about; here is someone with guts enough to ask me questions.* "Ask away," she said. It wasn't as easy as she thought.

"I was curious about those feathers on you?" The dove paused, and then added, "They're beautiful."

Leah couldn't believe her ears. Finally, someone who didn't mock her because she looked different. "You like them?" She spread her wings out, turning slowly to allow the dove to view them from all angles.

"Yes, I like them. But, can I ask another question...are you a sparrow?" The soft-spoken dove looked at her with wide-eyed curiosity.

Leah sighed. *Here I go. I should have known. I have to explain myself again.* "Yes, I'm a sparrow—a plain, little, brown Chipping Sparrow," she said in a sarcastic, monotone voice. "But, I decided that I wanted to look different, so I went after what I wanted. And, now, you're looking at it."

"I see. How in the world did you attach them to yourself?"

"I used some pine sap and glued them on. That's all. No big deal." She concluded that explaining herself to others was not fun.

"I see." The dove eyed Leah up and down again.

Leah felt her face burning red. With her chin jutted out, she said briskly, "I want to show everybody that a sparrow doesn't have to be plain and dull. Every one of these feathers represents something to me." As she pointed to each feather she kept an eye on the dove to catch her reaction. "The Jay's feather is for boldness. The Cardinal's feather is for distinction. The Yellow Warbler's feather is to sing just like them." She gave her head a hard nod, as though punctuating her good reasons with finality.

"I see," the dove said again, and giggled. "I'm sorry. I don't mean to laugh. It's just that I'm too cautious to be considered being bold, and I don't really know if that's good or not." She giggled again. "On the other hand, I've heard it said that being too bold is really being foolhardy. So, if being cautious is too limiting and being bold can be dangerous, what one's the best? I guess all I can say is wisdom helps us decide."

"What do you mean, wisdom helps you decide?" She wanted to hear what this dove had to say. There was a sort of knowing air surrounding this gentle, quiet bird.

"Well, let's see." The dove's head was tilted slightly, her eyes squinted. "Ok, one comes face to face with choices every day, right?"

"Right."

"Well, the one that decides against doing something dangerous, even if they think they can do it, that's wisdom. But, on the other hand, choosing to keep going without wisdom," the gray bird continued, "is right on course toward a head-on collision with life."

"But, we have to be bold and smart just to exist in this big, dangerous world as it is. It's all a head-on collision," she exclaimed, exasperation edging her voice. *I thought this nice bird was on my side.*

The dove looked right at Leah with intense black button eyes. "Wisdom doesn't come easily, little sparrow. One must work hard to gain wisdom to live strong and long in this world. It's not just about being smart and having boldness." She stopped as though to think a bit more. "You say boldness is why you got the Blue Jay's feather. Well, we both know about the Jay's rash intrusions on the rest of us birds just so he can get his fill first. Now, truthfully, how does that make you feel when he does that?"

"But, I got the Jay's feather for that exact reason, his commanding demeanor, whether I like his other character traits or not." Leah straightened up and squared her shoulders. "I fought hard to get them all." She vividly remembered the close calls, the struggles to glue them on, the dreadful dreams, the close death crashes into the water, the near-death experiences with Shadow and that large bird-thing, too. "I still choose to call myself bold instead of foolhardy."

"But where's the wisdom in it all if it almost costs you your life?"

Leah's mouth dropped open. "How did you know...?" She stopped. She wasn't about to reveal anything more to the dove.

"You were bold to be able to get what you wanted, but have you really thought it through whether it's been good for you?" she cooed softly. "Boldness is good when wisdom is its partner. Without that partnership, boldness is just plain reckless and dangerous."

The words cut through Leah's heart like a knife. But, stubbornness clung to her like the dried-out oak leaves still clinging to the trees in her woods. "Well, I've grown accustomed to these feathers. I settle them into my own feathers so I can fly, including adjusting my flight pattern so I don't get too exhausted. I believe that's called wisdom. To be able to adjust to something that's different is pretty bold, if you ask me."

"But, are you living the life you were given to live as a sparrow, like your own Chipping Sparrow clan? For that matter, with the entire natural kingdom—the Humankind included? Even a sparrow has a specific place and a purpose in this world."

Leah didn't answer. The dove prepared to fly away, but before she did she gave Leah something else to think about. "One day Wisdom, Brave Wisdom, will show you, little Chipping Sparrow." With a sort of pleading in her voice, she added, "Please, take care of yourself."

The dove flew off with the trademark whistling sound of her wings trailing behind her. Leah stood staring at the lone figure disappearing over tall trees north of her. She wasn't sure if she was angry or awestruck by all the words spoken from the dove. Her thoughts were stirred away from the sky as she noticed rabbits feeding close by. They stood on their hind legs as though waiting to see what she would do next. Leah opened her wings and retreated into the heights of the cotton-clouded sky. She was reeling from the conversation with the dove.

*What in the world did she mean by "Brave Wisdom will show me someday?" Who, or what, is that?* She heaved a tired sigh. *Oh, it doesn't matter. It doesn't matter what others think of me, either. I'm going to go on doing what I think is best. Best for me.*

But the dove's words rang in her ears like the constant buzzing of a cicada; one could hear it, but one could not get rid of it.

Fields of winter wheat were fully grown and dense in late summer. Black and white dairy cattle spotted the emerald landscape as they wandered through the pastures, lazily feeding on the lush grass; their growing calves followed close behind. Leah continued flying passed more fields and farms until they began to disappear from sight. She heard the distinct high-pitched peals of the seagulls. The Big Waters was now close.

Lifting higher over a swell of trees, she saw the horizon stretching out as far as the eye could see, out into the mystical gray-blue water where it disappeared into the skyline. The sheen from flying seagulls came into view as sunrays bounced off their sleek white bodies. The squawking banter grew louder as it crossed the vast blueness.

Many gulls were busily stirring over land and water, and Leah could see why. The beach was active with humans. The day's hot sun and cool water brought them out to the water's edge. The children's high energetic sounds challenged the noise level of the gulls as small waves crashed into their sun-reddened bodies.

An elderly couple sat together on a colorful striped blanket, separated from the rest of the noisy crowd, an open picnic basket between them. Both had gray hair, although the woman covered hers in a wide-brimmed hat as shade from the sun. The man held onto a string that extended into the sky as a brightly painted kite sailed with its tail swirling and fishtailing elegantly in the wind. The couple laughed and talked excitedly as they watched their paper amusement stay up in the invisible billows of air.

Leah descended onto a branch of a fallen tree trunk weathered gray and smooth by the constant blowing sands. She would observe all the activities of the seagulls from this vantage point for that one sure opportunity to help gain a new feather. Right away she spotted a particular seagull that was slowly circling a fishing boat. Someone from the boat tossed food overboard. The gull instantly turned sharply and dove for it. Just as quickly, a dozen other gulls converged on the same spot like a white cloud falling down from the sky. Whatever was tossed over was gone in seconds. The greedy birds lifted up out of the water again to continue scavenging somewhere else. But, the first gull remained.

Leah shifted her sights back to the couple who had anchored the kite in the sand. They opened their picnic basket and began to pull out their lunch. After a short time of munching on a sandwich, the woman tossed away the leftovers only a few feet behind them. Unbelievably, not a single gull noticed. Leah quickly grasped onto her lucky opportunity. She flew to inspect what was discarded in hopes it was something of great value.

"Good! It's bread." Leah chirped out in joy.

The man looked back just in time to see the sparrow reaching for the piece of bread.

WINGS FOR LEAH SPARROW

"Look at that, Mildred," he whispered. "A little sparrow just came after that piece of bread you threw out."

"I see that, Harold," the woman responded quietly, her eyes turned into slits as she tried to focus. "That's strange. Are you sure that's a sparrow? It has very peculiar feathers on it for a sparrow, don't you think?"

"Come to think of it, it does. I've never seen anything like that before. Do you think someone caught it and played some joke on it?"

"I wish I knew. That poor little thing probably struggles with all those different feathers on it. I mean, it seems to me that they would be very hard for something as tiny as that little bird to carry."

"Well, however it happened, I hope they come off soon or it might not survive."

"I sure hope so, too."

Leah, of course, did not understand the concern the humans directed toward her. She only knew one thing. She picked up the morsel of soft bread and quickly flew back to the big driftwood. It was tasty, something she would have quickly eaten herself. But this piece of bread was going to be the lure she needed to attract an unsuspecting seagull.

She decided it was better to be farther away from the commotion on the beach. Away from the congregating gulls that, like radar, picked up on the people's noontime lunch. Many of the birds landed on the sand, sneaking up as close as was comfortable, waiting for any tidbit tossed out to them. Children begged their parents for anything to throw out to the gulls, giggling at the scurrying that ensued for the food. Humans were generous with food and the seagull's high screeches rang out as reminders not to forget about them.

Leah flew a great distance down the beach, passed a barking, ball-chasing dog and its human. Dogs didn't overly concern Leah. They weren't fast enough to catch birds, but they were enough of a nuisance to stay clear of them. Landing on a line of wayward scrub brushes that topped a four-foot sand hill sloping away from the beach, Leah could clearly see the lone seagull still waiting for any handouts thrown from the boat. A game plan was formed and she once again flew high above the beach, casting a quick glance at the many other hungry gulls still engrossed with the humans. She hovered for a few seconds making sure the lone seagull would get a good eye view of her bait. She dropped the delicacy to the ground and dashed back into the bushes.

The keen eyesight of the seagull caught the movement. With effortless flaps of his wings, he skimmed inches above the water smoothly and evenly. At times the tips of his wings lightly touched the water like a perfect skipping stone. He reached the spot quickly and hungrily pounced on the piece of bread.

Leah had to act fast if she was going to get a feather from this seagull. She forgot what voracious eaters gulls were, but remembered to be careful around them. They were hyper quarrelsome birds, and could easily eat any small injured bird, because, after all, they were scavengers. Leah flew to just a few feet away from the dining gull and cautiously began inching her way toward him.

"Mr. Seagull, could I have a few words with you, please?" She continued toward the white bird in slow steps. "I dropped that piece of bread especially for you." A little quiver of fear escaped from her voice. She hoped the gull hadn't detected it. *Is this brave wisdom or stupid boldness?*

She felt incredibly small when the big gull pulled itself up after consuming the meal. He was at least three times larger than she was—a creature she never dreamed to make her acquaintance. In the vivid sun, its pure white body secured an energetic radiance, with its wings standing a pale gray against it. Its large yellow hooked bill had a black band going around the tip. The seagull looked squarely at Leah with its round, yellow orbs as though she could be his next course for dinner.

*Does he think I'm an injured bird?* She began to back away ever so slightly.

The seagull suddenly squawked so loud that Leah bolted backwards, losing her footing. She scrambled to her feet, keeping her eyes on the gull. She didn't realize the seagull's cry at such close range was so torturous to the ears.

"Oh, so you think I should thank you," the seagull said sarcastically.

"Well, I could have easily eaten it myself, sir."

"I assure you that I would have found some food sooner or later without your help, little bird. I scavenge for my food all the time. Alone," he boomed, emphasizing the last word strongly.

"Yes, I understand. But, didn't you like it sooner than later?"

The seagull stared at Leah, again making her feel uneasy that she went down on her haunches in case she had to make a fast move and fly away.

"Ha-ha-ha!" the seagull screeched abruptly. "You're right. You did save me some unnecessary wing flaps, I suppose." He again stared at Leah, but this time it was as though he was seeing her for the first time. "Who are you...or rather...what are you?" the gull asked, cocking his head to one side and then another, taking her in from different angles. "You are rather alien-looking. But, I must say that you do have the look of a regular sparrow," he mused, not giving Leah time to answer him. "Huh. It's strange how I travel far and wide and have seen some rather bizarre things in my lifetime, and eaten some, too, but I don't think I've ever seen anything like you."

116

"Yes, well, I am a regular sparrow, as you say." Her words had an edge of tenseness in them. *How many times do I have to explain myself to others?* "But, Mr. Seagull, I'm here to ask for one small favor in return for the bread I found for you." She cleared her throat. "Could I please have one of your feathers? I've seen your kind fly. I've seen you glint in the sky like shining silver, so white and so beautiful."

Rude and unrefined as gulls could be, not paying much attention to Leah, the gull groomed his feathers as she spoke.

"Sir? Sir! Did you hear me?"

The seagull stopped sprucing up and yawned. "What? Oh, you. Yes, I heard you. But, the fact that you provided a morsel for me and that you admire my feathers and that we are talking together does not mean that I am in a giving mood. I don't go around doing what others ask of me, especially when it comes to giving something of mine away. You see, I usually take what I need, especially when I'm hungry."

*Oh, no. Where am I going to find another piece of food to wrestle a feather from this stingy bird? Stay calm, Leah, you need this feather.* Leah straightened up in hopes of adding a little more bravado to her tiny stature as she faced the large scavenger-bird. "I came a long way here to ask a favor from you, Mr. Seagull. I hope I didn't waste my time in coming here and finding you that piece of food without at least having the decency of you giving me your attention."

The gull found himself struck by the fact that a mini-bird dared come close to him for anything at all, let alone to ask for one of his feathers. Slightly intrigued with this bizarre contest of the wills, and also for the makings of an extraordinary story for his treasure-trove of wayfaring adventures to tell other gull cousins, the large bird began to rethink his decision.

"I do admit I have to give you credit for bravery to approach a bigger and better bird than you. You seem to possess some mental capability to have grabbed my attention from the water with that piece of food." He paused as he searched the inquisitive face of the little sparrow in front of him. "But, you do know my feathers are way too large for you, don't you? You're not that stupid, are you?"

Leah again tightened her jaw to keep from spitting out what she truly thought about this filthy scrounger that, without a shadow of a doubt, outnumbered her scathing opinions about the odious characteristics of the Blue Jay.

"Yes, I know they're larger. But, I only want a small one."

The seagull looked out to the water toward the fishing boat, anxious to get back to the business of what gulls do best, foraging. With signs of growing impatience, the seagull spoke briskly. "Oh, all right! I suppose you can have one. What do I care what you do with your life."

"Thank you, sir! Thank you so very much."

"I'll give you one closer to your size. It'll still have that same glint, as you call it, as the rest of my other feathers," he said, pulling out a smaller feather from higher up his wing. He dropped it onto the warm sand in front of him. "Does that suit you?"

"Yes! Yes it does," Leah cried out excitedly. She didn't move toward the feather. For all she knew, it could be a trick to grab her as she reached for it.

"Well, what are you waiting for?" the gull spit out impatiently. "Are you going to take it, or not?"

"Yes, I am." But, again, she stood still, keeping a watchful eye on every move he made.

"Oh, I see. You don't trust me, do you?" he asked, watching Leah back away even farther. "I don't blame you!" he squawked out with laughter. He prepared to fly away. Looking at the confused array of feathers on Leah, a mischievous smirk crossed his face. "Well, little bird, I hope you don't ever desire a turkey's feather," he said as he jumped up into the air. He began a slow, circling ascent above her.

"A turkey's feather?" Leah's head turned upwards, making sure the seagull was staying up. "Why would I want a turkey's feather?" she asked. "Turkeys don't fly!"

"Exactly!" the gull cackled, and like a flash he was over the blue water, raucous laughter trailing him. In no time, the brash white bird was sailing around the boat that had putted farther out into the horizon.

Leah held a quizzical look on her face as she stared long after it, a tiny white spot in the gray-blue sky. Suddenly, her mouth dropped open. Anger pierced her mind. "How dare he make fun of me. I'll show him."

Leah picked up her possession and flew away from the beach with very little peace in her heart. She didn't like the gull at all or what he had insinuated to her about the turkey feather. It hurt her, but she held on to the promise she made to herself. She was about to know a new dimension with this feather. It was called freedom. She had long admired the seagull's ease in flying and slicing so gracefully through the air, then, expertly jack-knifing into another turn. The way they hovered above the earth and water so easily as though stopped in time, their wings outstretched, held magically by the constant gusts of the wind above the sea was all a wonder to her. But, the main reason for all this madness was the feather's witness in the sunshine. That's what she called freedom. Freedom is what she wanted in her life; freedom to fly freely and expertly. She would not be so easily missed in the big sky with a gleaming silvery feather of her own.

# Chapter 11

# THE RESCUE

*For he will put his angels in charge of you;*
*To guard you in all your ways. They shall bear you up.*
*- Psalms 91*

Leah was quite aware of the long flight home. With the seagull feather length-wise across her beak, flying was much restrained. Exhaustion came too quickly in the late afternoon and she needed to do something to help ease the pressure. She settled to travel the shorter route home, the best way to get there before dusk. That meant by way of the horse farm, the one place she avoided on her way to the Big Waters. But, there was no other alternative. The farther route home meant traveling until close to dark or staying overnight at a strange place. Leah was not too keen with either idea.

The strong wind from the Big Waters was now a gentle whisper at the church grounds she was entering, yet it was enough to stir fresh fragrances emitting from the maturing flora. Butterflies bounced around a heavily-laden flowering bush and hornets found fine clay for building hives under an overflowing flower basket. The garden was alive with the summer's attractive days. No humans were present to disturb the kingdom of animals that appeared quietly behind the church.

Leah tucked the gull feather underneath her wing and perched on a feeder to begin her meal. But she quickly became aware of a sound that she hadn't heard in her other visits: rushing water. She went to investigate. The garden was built in a circular fashion with walkways crisscrossing it. Surrounded by a covering of flowers, plants and shrubs, was a small fishpond. A smaller upper-level pool circulated the water over the ledge and into the larger pool creating a waterfall, thus affecting the sound Leah heard.

She stood on a miniature tree that overlooked the water and saw a group of plump golden fish swimming around. She had never seen such bright fish before. The only kind she was familiar with was small silver ones in her pond, nabbed by visiting heron for food. Those fish were tiny and gray...just like her. These gold fish were considerably different. So impressive were the fish to her that she yielded herself even more so to the compelling idea that different is good, and good for being noticed.

"Those fish look incredible," she whispered. She continued watching them as they glided smoothly through the water; their long, flowing tails waved like sheer curtains behind them. Leah noticed that the fish would come to the top and nibble at anything that happened to fall into the water: a bug, a piece of a torn leaf, a flower's peddle, all dropping down from the halting breeze. "I wonder if those fish think everything that hits the water is food."

Leah noticed a clearing behind the waterfall where the lower ledge caught just enough splashes from the falls and made a nice sized nook to bathe in. "Good. Just what I need; a cool splash on a hot day." With the seagull feather back in her beak, she made her way to the landing on the ledge of the cascading falls. The goldfish had retreated across the way to some movement on the water. Leah was satisfied they weren't close to her side of the pond.

As she lowered herself into the water, the usual chain of thoughts and strategies came to mind about attaching the newest feather onto her. Tomorrow she would have full possession of the seagull feather as her very own. She dipped into the water, shaking and splashing to completely get soaked. She felt the coolness soothe her tired body. Then a frightening thought barged into her rest. There were small rocks situated throughout the nook where she stood and pictures of a snake entered her mind gripping her with fear. But, she quickly stopped herself.

"Wait! Think about it, Leah. A snake would be too big to hide behind these small rocks. No way could they coil up small enough to fit into this tight spot." She took a few deep breaths. "I hope not, anyway." She splashed about in the water again, spraying her body and wings with the cool wetness, as much to clear her mind as to feel energized. She filled with pride as she felt boldness rise in her that could only be attributed to her Blue Jay feather. "I wish that dove was here to see me now. She would see in me that boldness that we talked about. What a shocker it'd be to her, too, when I'd tell her how I got my Seagull feather!"

Her words hardly left her mouth when something from behind struck her with such force that it knocked her forward, narrowly pushing her over the ledge and into the bigger pool. The hard hit forced her mouth open as breath escaped, and the seagull feather dropped into the water. She watched in dismay as the feather twirled around in circles in the strong current and away from her. But, she was in a lot more trouble than losing a feather.

Whatever held her was holding her fast by the foot. Her mind dashed about in alarm as she struggled to get away, but to no avail. She beat her wings against the ledge for leverage to break free, only succeeding in tiring herself. Finally, mustering everything from inside her, she turned to look at the attacker. To her astonishment, holding her by its huge mouth was a large fat bullfrog.

*A frog! I can't believe my eyes! A frog! Frogs eat birds? What in the world am I going to do?* Again she fought viciously, using her wings, hoping the commotion would frighten the bullfrog and let her go. But, it didn't work. Yet, the hungry amphibian had not grabbed her any tighter, either. Survival instincts kicked in once again. *It makes me cringe just thinking about being in this green monster's mouth for even one second longer, but when the warty frog opens its mouth to get a better hold of me, I'll escape from its jaws. I just have to wait for the right moment. It has to work. It just has to!*

As best as she could, she stretched out toward the edge of the nook in hopes that as soon as she felt any sort of tension loosened, she would make a fast break for it. That was her plan, anyway. She was exhausted from the first attempt to escape her captor, but she knew the bullfrog would have to make a move again soon. It was imperative that she lay still to force the amphibian to make the first move.

Leah was right. The frog opened his mouth to adjust its hold on his quarry. In the split second she felt the slight pressure ease off her leg, she yanked herself free, instantly springing forward. But, to her dismay, the deluge of the waterfall knocked her right down into the fishpond. Leah had not anticipated the intensity of the falls to over-power her. She went underwater for a split second, but she battled to the top again, away from its force. Sputtering for breath, more panic set in; the bullfrog could jump in after her. This was his domain. Leah struck her wings on the water to stay afloat, sapping more strength all too quickly. Adding to the shock, she remembered about the goldfish.

"Oh, no! Those goldfish could easily think I'm food and nibble me to death." Yet, a faint glimmer of hope slowly made its way into her world of chaos. "Maybe since I'm close to the noisy falls, it camouflages any unusual sounds coming from me struggling in the water." She was well aware that this hope was like a rope made out of a spider's web; very thin, indeed.

Treading farther away from the ledge where she hoped the frog had stayed, she saw something long and white floating up next to her. It was her seagull feather. Without hesitation she grasped it and continued to float. She was totally spent. She wasn't only dealing with physical exhaustion, but also the mental anguish of the wait. Waiting for something to come after her from above the water or below it was exhaustion to the extreme. She had no life-saving ideas to get her out of another mess should the frog decide to chase down his food that got away. Her mind was tired of thinking. Her wings were spread out like floats; she knew it was now only a short time before the water would submerge them and her. She would drop peacefully to the bottom of the pond without anything else in the world to have to worry about.

*I just want to rest...that's all...just rest and sleep.*

As she kicked her legs to elevate herself a little longer, she saw a shadow come over her. She recalled a far-away memory, fresh out of her egg-womb, a similar thing happened. A shadow had obscured the warmth of the sum from her after appearing naked into the world. She then heard a loving and familiar voice, "Yes, she's a runt, alright." How she wished she could see her father again. Leah was in limbo, withdrawn from the horror of her situation, retreating far into the recesses of her mind. Resigning herself to that poignant image in her mind, all she had to do was go to sleep in the cool watery bed. The water covered her face. The Seagull's feather swirled away.

"Oh, you poor little birdie!"

A blurry, watery image appeared before Leah's eyes as a shadowy figure reach down into the water and scooped her up.

"Grandma! Grandma! Look. A poor little bird drowned in the pond." It was the voice of a little human, barely audible to Leah's waterlogged ears. It seemed so far away, like a soft echo in a hollowed-out log. "Come quick, Grandma." There was some jostling as the human opened up her warm hands to show the wet shivering bird to a larger human close to her.

"Oh, my goodness." A little shock wave of concern spirited toward Leah as the bigger human took her from the small hands. More warmth encircled her, more jostling came, and Leah found herself wrapped in something soft that smelled like flowers. Her view became gray again.

"No, it's not dead, sweetie, but how in the world did this little thing end up in the fish pond? It's a good thing I came to work in the garden at church today and brought you along with me. It might have been too late for this little bird. You saved its life, Jessica."

"How neat, Grandma. I was just coming to see the goldfish when I saw it in the water. Then it started sinking. I just had to do something."

The voice of the smaller human sounded just as Leah had heard them speak before, high-pitched and full of spirit and energy. The heat engulfed her, radiating from the cupped hands gently holding her through the mild-scented material. It reminded her of the times her mother's warm body shielded her against blustering cold rainstorms.

"Don't be afraid, little bird," cooed the older voice. "I'm just going to dry you up a bit. You're soaked through. How you ended up in the pond is beyond me. But, you're safe now. We'll make sure of that. We promise, right, Jessica?"

"We sure do, little birdie."

"Let's take it home with us. Then, we'll see if it can fly again."

"You think I can keep it, Grandma? I mean, I did find it and save its life."

"Oh, no, honey. Wild birds are meant to be free. They can't be caged up. They'd die, no matter how careful you are with them."

"Oh. I wouldn't want that. It almost died just a little bit ago."

"Yes, almost, but you came to its rescue."

Something about that gentle older voice sounded very familiar to Leah. The humans continued talking, carefully patting dry the little bird. The three of them began moving away from the garden. Leah could tell because the waterfall's gurgling faded away as they withdrew. She was surprised about the turn of events. The way the humans were speaking to her, so soothingly, so warmly, was one reason fear was not screaming in her. After all, she was alive. The older human's voice came again, and once again Leah sought deep into her memory for something she knew she'd heard before. She allowed that it reminded her of a dove's soft, low cooing.

*That's it! I remember. It's the white-haired lady from the feast garden…the one with the two apple trees. I know it's her. She's the one that comes out to feed us and talks to us birds. She's the one with that soft voice, the one I always like to listen to, the one that sounds like a dove.*

Still, even in the stark reality about her find, Leah felt the weight of the horrendous episode begin to sweep over her like lead weight. With the gentle sound of the older woman, the slow beat of the walk, and the cozy cover over her, Leah suddenly felt very drowsy. She was surprised how trusting she felt toward this human. That quirky little hummingbird and the trust it demonstrated toward her human, Leah remembered thinking that she didn't have the capacity to trust anyone that way. The trio stopped and the woman opened the covering.

"If I didn't know any better," the older woman said, "I'd say you were a sparrow. But, it's beyond me how those colorful feathers managed to get stuck on you. Let's see here..."

Leah felt a gentle tug on her wing of the Yellow Warbler feather as the woman attempted to pull it off. Leah didn't protest this time. She recalled her vehement protest, so long ago it seemed, when her sparrow cousin tried to do the same. Surprisingly, she felt comfortable with the woman's tender touch.

*My seagull feather! Oh, no, after all that hard work, I lost my seagull feather.*

It was yet another tragic loss to endure: no adorning herself with that elusive silver gleam of the gull's feather. The one redeeming factor for this long tiring day was the fact that she had outsmarted both the seagull and the bullfrog.

After trying unsuccessfully to pull off the tuft, the older woman said, "Oh, well, I'll just let things be seeing as they are pretty stuck on you. But, I guess I'll never know how they got on you in the first place. I just hope no one was up to some mischief."

The woman walked along slowly, the little girl with quicker steps to keep up. Leah had no idea where these humans were taking her, but she was willing to believe she was safe, in any case. A soft jostling and a muffled thud startled her. The human had closed a door, a motor started up, and she heard the familiar rumbling noise she's heard many times on the roads the people traveled. She then felt the bundle she was encased in held firmly and, in a smooth movement, they drove away from the church. Leah lay with her tired eyes closed making it easier for her to quiet her spirit in much-needed rest.

Suddenly, she heard a high-pitched tune whistled over and over; three short low notes ending with three rapid high notes in a row. Leah immediately recognized it. It was the song she had coveted from the Yellow Warbler she chased into the woods.

"Wow, Grandma. That was neat."

"Thank you, Jessica," she said with a soft chuckle. "Well, sweetie, I feed them all the time and I listen to them, too. So, I've practiced their songs for a long time. How does that sound to you, little sparrow? I'm sure I don't sound as beautiful as the Yellow Warbler, but I do try. Now, let's see, here's another one I try to imitate."

The woman whistled again. This one began with a high pitched note, dipping to a low one, and finished with three higher fast ones. She repeated it a few times.

*She's trying to communicate with me. I have no idea what she's saying, but that's close to the sound of the Chickadee.* Leah was surprised what the human was doing.

"Did you like that one, birdie? That one is from the Chickadee. Oh, what a funny little thing to watch. They're so cute, and they're not afraid of me when I come close to feed all of you birds. They even come right next to me and feed at the feeders as I fill other ones. They like to keep me company. I sure like that about them."

"Can I try one of them, Grandma?"

"Well, sure you can. Here, listen to it and then try yourself," said the woman, as she mimicked a Chickadee again. "Now, you try it."

Leah then heard a hodgepodge of notes that hurt her ears. *It certainly is no bird I've ever heard before.*

"I messed up big time," the girl said, chuckling.

"Well, keep practicing, honey. That's all it takes."

Leah felt the blanket she was bundled in begin to move slightly. A hole appeared right above her head. She could now look out from a small opening right to a small human face. The girl smiled at her.

"It sure is a pretty little thing, Grandma. What kind of bird did you say it was?"

"Now, I'm guessing it's a sparrow, even with those odd feathers attached to it, but I don't know exactly what family it's from. There are many, many different types of sparrows. Seeing as it's brown and seems smaller than other sparrows, I'd guess that it is a Chipping Sparrow. I'm not really sure, though. But, in any case, even with all those colorful feathers on it, it's still the same sweet little bird it was created to be," the woman cooed. "I do so love all kinds of birds. They are what fill my days with joy now that I'm all alone." The lady began her soft songs again. Leah listened until the accumulated heat in the bunched up sweater and the tiny rocking motion underneath her from a caring little girl took her into another fast sleep.

The car came to a stop and the engine was cut off. Leah woke up with a new concern: she didn't know if she was going to be set free. The caged bird she'd once seen, unable to fly but from wall to wall of that prison, made Leah's mind race with renewed anxiety.

*What if the humans want to keep me as a pet like those house birds? I couldn't live that way. I've got to try to escape as soon as possible. I don't belong inside a human's nest-home.*

The older woman cooed soft sounds to Leah as she picked the sparrow up from her granddaughter's arms. They walked to the back yard. Carefully, she lay Leah down on a wooden picnic table. Both humans carefully unraveled the sweater until only Leah's head showed. The clear blue sky appeared above her, something Leah didn't think she'd ever see again. Instantly, she smelled the sweet aroma of roses and the earthy scent of freshly mown grass. Leah then heard a most welcoming sound: the singing and calling of her fellow birds.

"I think you're pretty much over that horrendous experience you had, you poor little thing. You're almost dry, too." She lifted Leah out of the warm cocoon. Tenderly, she cupped Leah in her soft, velvety hands. "What a day we've all had today. But, it looks like we're none the worse for it. Right, Jessica?"

"Right, Grandma. I'm sure glad we were able to save it and help it get better."

"So am I."

Leah lay without moving a muscle; she really didn't know why. She had told herself that she was going to fly away the first chance she got, but she didn't. She kept listening to the calm voice speaking to her, feeling a tenderness emitting from human to animal. She found herself resting easily in the old wrinkled hands.

Once again, the woman examined Leah as she spoke. "Hm-m. You definitely are a sparrow. I can see that for sure now. But it seems as though someone got the notion to make you into something you're not. What a shame," she said with a click of her tongue. "I don't under-stand the cruelty of some people these days. Oh, well," she sighed, "since we can't take these feathers off of you, and you seem to have survived, I guess you'll be just fine." The woman opened her cupped hands slightly to let what little pressure she held on Leah ease up. "I do hope you know that your kind is the most versatile bird in the bird kingdom. Sparrows can live anywhere. The Bible says, 'The sparrow has found a home, a place near your altar, O God.' Isn't that beautiful? They must be very special if the Creator has them near him. I believe that's called real love. It would be a pretty dull place without sparrows in the world. Don't you ever forget that, you pretty little thing."

Leah found herself sitting on opened palms. No sweater covered her, no fingers held her down. She was, basically, free to go. Facing the kindly lady with the light-brown eyes and a dove's soft voice, seeing the shorter human standing beside her, she again surprised herself by remaining where she was. She should be retreating as fast as she could. But wisdom (and she knew it must be the wisdom the dove talked to her about) seemed to whisper its gentle nudge in her spirit, telling her that she was safe with them. It wasn't foolhardy staying just a little bit longer, nor was it boldness, either. It was trust. She had been shown great care, compassion, and love in her time of need and she believed she learned a little bit of what the tiny Hummingbird mother was trying to explain to a shocked sparrow back then.

"Go on, little sparrow," the woman said, giving her hands a little upward shove to encourage Leah. "You're free to go. You belong out there in that great big beautiful world. There's plenty of room for you and everyone else. So spread your wings…and fly!"

Leah flew away.

"Bye, little birdie. Take care of yourself," the child's voice cried out.

# Chapter 12

# FOLLOWING THE CALL

*Who hath ears to hear, let him hear.*
*Mark 4:9*

Leah was right. She recognized the place flying away from the human's home. It was her favorite feast garden with the two apple trees, now filled with hundreds of red apples ready for the picking. For a little while, she had been in the human's world in a very unexpected and close-up encounter, a meeting Leah would never have thought possible. Surviving after being held by a human? Yet, in the bizarre twist of fate, it was her salvation.

She let out a big sigh of relief. She was home. It felt so good to see her familiar surroundings. Settling down for a long needed rest, Leah looked at the dark water rippling softly in the pond, sparkling from the rising pale moon's gleam. The frogs were harmonious again tonight, something Leah had never minded before. They were sounds she always connected with home—hypnotic and untamed music. Yet, after today's harrowing escape from the bullfrog's mouth, she wasn't sure whether she would ever see them in the same way again.

"It's amazing how one can see things so differently from what they really are. That fishpond at the church was so beautiful, so full of wonderful things. The fish were so graceful in the water, the waterfall so tranquil. The flowers, the plants, my feather…" Leah winced once more as she remembered the disappointment of losing her seagull feather. "It all seemed such a perfect world, but it almost became a watery grave for me. I was almost frog fodder. I would never have guessed that a bug-eating creature would go for flesh and feathers. I used to think that they were just green, harmless, hoppy things. What an eye-opener. Now here I am at home, hearing them again in the pond. They must multiply by the millions. I'll certainly have to be more careful next time I go to the water—if I ever go there again."

Leah's thoughts trailed off to the beat of the frogs croaking and the higher pitches of their smaller cousins, the peepers, thousands of them it seemed to her. But, even with the recent knowledge of the frog's true colors, Leah found herself falling asleep to their rapport. Yet, sleep was not the restful escape she had wanted. Quick flashes of frog's mouths and harsh croaks startled her many times. A dreamy scene of the waterfall that knocked her down into near oblivion shook her awake and she heard an incredible sound. A sound she's heard twice before; she was sure of it. The explosive peal still ringing in her ears, Leah woke up panting for air the same way she did when the little human fished her out of the pond. Daylight hit her face, bringing her back to reality and to another day where the early morning's activities and noise fully awakened her.

Leah felt a heaviness of dread on her chest. Something bothered her. There was no joy like she had when searching for her feathers.

Looking back to everything she had endured for them, the waiting, the anticipation, the hard work to accomplish all she had set out to do, she felt even more anxious. Physically she was totally spent. What little rest she did get wasn't enough. She hadn't eaten right in days, something a bird cannot do. Even the Cardinal's feather tuft on top of her head weighed like a thousand pounds of bricks.

A stirring of the wind on the full trees around her sounded like hisses of a snake. A pair of Blue Jays nearby screeched loudly as though they were cackling out hateful words, words *she* even believed about her.

"Loser! Loser! Loser!"

The day had begun in a dim, silvery aura. Dim, like she felt. Even with the second chance at life she received when she was saved by the humans she felt despair for what she didn't have, what she couldn't be, and what she'd tried to change, yet failed to achieve.

"Oh, how I wish that huge bird was here." Leah gasped. "What am I saying? That thing almost *killed* me! Well, no, not really. But it almost *ate* me. Well, no, it didn't do that either." Leah sat contemplating about the giant enigma she had involuntarily encountered. "Why does that thing always seem to be around me at a crucial point in my life?"

As though in answer to her question, a fearsome cry suddenly echoed like thunder through the woods. Everything—the frogs, the chattering Blue Jays sitting on the treetops, the ranting squirrels, and even the now older ducklings and their parents—went deafeningly quiet. Leah instantly recognized the voice, and she knew in her heart that the voice was specifically calling her. She didn't understand how she knew it, but the only thing she wanted to see more than anything else in her life was the owner of that voice.

*Leah! Leah!*

The sound reverberated smoothly, dwindling eastward. It was leaving her woods. Without a second thought, Leah shot out of her nest and went in the direction of the call. She had an overwhelming desire to follow it. Something inside of her felt urgent.

As the wind whipped around her ears, Leah focused hard, hoping to hear it once more. She no longer doubted that this huge voice, which had exploded into her small world, was speaking directly to her. It was a mystifying voice; one in which she didn't hear battering words leveled at her, or mocking words that caused her to recoil in excruciating pain. It wasn't like other voices that so insidiously made their way into her mind and spirit like the great force of driving sand; irritating, wearing down her resolve. She didn't hear condemnation or warped laughter. She didn't feel abused or belittled. This massive commanding voice, grand yet fearsome as it was, had almost become a portent of goodness to her. It was to her like the human lady's cooing voice, a sort of reassurance that someone was there to care for her, to help her.

Leah continued her pondering and her flying. But, she had no idea if she was following the right way. It was toward the Big Waters, but in a more northeasterly direction. She was heading towards the mountains! The mountains of very high terrain, a higher area than any of her kind flew normally. Mountains manifested in her mind as a wholly unusual and much more dangerous place than where she lived.

"The voice faded in that direction. I'm sure of it."

Leah was tiring. The quick decision to follow the stranger didn't leave any time for her to look for food. It had been a while since she had eaten anything, and she needed energy now. But, suddenly, new energy surged through her as she again heard the cry. She had been right; it was coming from the shadowy mountains looming straight ahead of her, north along the Big Waters.

"It's like he wants me to follow him."

Leah continued her journey northeast, again without food or rest. She was far behind whatever it was she was following. Certainly no distance flyer compared to that massive bird, but Leah had no intention of losing him. The landscape changed drastically as she left her familiar territory behind. She was entering an enormous forested area stretching as far as the eye could see, a formidable green sea of trees, save for the outcropping of the mammoth mountains miles ahead. There were fewer signs of the humankind here. No fields or pasture animals, no farms or farmhouses. There were also no noticeable roads. What she did see was a very dense fortress, and above that the skyline of the high, blue-gray mounds stretching upwards. She was almost sure the bird ahead of her lived there. It had to. Where else could a monstrous bird like that live?

But, now Leah felt her traveling time was coming to an end. She had to stop whether she liked it or not, and it was going to be in the darkness of this extraordinarily widespread woodland.

## *Chapter 13*

# THE DEEP GREEN FOREST

*In the hour of adversity be not without hope,*
*For crystal rain falls from black clouds.*
*-Nizami*

Patches of charcoal gray clouds dotting the sky spelled out a gloomy day. As soon as Leah entered the forest a light haziness enveloped her. Mother Nature's attitude was something she could hardly prevent. The resulting hot days mixed with the cooler woods captured lush forest life in thin, misty layers of vapor.

Leah stopped on a low thick branch and searched the ground for food. With great relief she spotted a meal under a small fruit-bearing tree. Where much fruit was, there would be congregating insects, also. She scanned the area before heading down. Thick vines with tiny leaves clung to the trees, extending from the ground across to the very tops as though reaching for as much growth-giving light as possible, stretching a verdant curtain across the trees like green lace.

*One would have to be very careful flying around here. Someone could fly right into those intertwining vines and get pretty stuck.* She flew to the ground and picked on the mixture of food in front of her as she continued contemplating her destination. *I'm going to lose more time. I'm pretty far behind already, but at least I've got the general direction.* She looked through the dark, dense trees. *I guess I'll have to go through there.*

The forest was so large and widespread that it stretched for miles to the north and east to the Big Waters. *I've just got to catch up to... Who is it? Why do I even want to see it? He frightened me to death the first time. Why do I want to meet up with him now?* Yet with all the perturbing doubts rolling around her head, Leah felt an unbelievable excitement mounting up inside of her, and she couldn't shake it off. *For whatever the reason, though, I've just got to find him. That's all there is to it.* She recognized her need to find this creature was as deep a longing in her as when she desired to search out a feather; motivation at its helm.

Leah left the food and began the long trek through the forest. She was more comfortable closer to the ground for safety reasons—the chance of any attack would not be as easy. Every once in a while she went over the top of the trees to check her location and see how much closer she was to her intended target: the mountains.

She encountered many birds in the vast woodland, many of the same species that lived in her own home area. She easily noticed the Cardinals with their outstanding color, the black and gray Chickadees, all busily flying about. She also saw squirrels and chipmunks and heard the noisy shrieks of the Blue Jays that echoed through the lush, green barrier. Leah ventured to guess these forested animals were accustomed to the natural way of feeding themselves without provision from other means, not at all used to the humans like she was. It was written in their make-up, their inbred nature, and the way of survival for any animal that lived far away from the human populace. There were no free handouts here.

Leah heard a loud gurgling sound come from below her as she continued through the woods. She stopped on a large oak and hid behind its thick leaves watching in amazement as a rather enormous bird crashed out of a thicket and quickly ascended onto the branch of a nearby tree. Her heart skipped a beat as she immediately thought it was the bird-stranger she was chasing. But she recognized by the dark coloring and bulky torso that it was a wild turkey. It gobbled excitedly as it checked out the culprit that made it leave the ground and flee to safety.

A raccoon scrambled out of the same thicket where the ruffled turkey had been seconds before. Raccoons especially loved eggs, and the mother turkey was now watching helplessly as the villain stole away with one of her eggs in its mouth. Her discovered nest would not be safe anymore. Leah set out once more, leaving the sad sight of the mother turkey unsure of what to do.

Leah caught grasshoppers and fed on insects along her route toward the mountains. The small intakes of food were the energy she needed to keep going. Yet, what she needed most was Herculean strength. Energy was one thing, but strength was another. It was what she needed now to keep on searching for that dark peculiar bird. It was inner strength she needed to keep her mind steady on what she was doing and why. Her thoughts puzzled her. They had taken a sharp detour from her all-consuming penchant for adorning her lack-luster life, remembering how important it had been to collect the colorful treasures in the first place. Now it was like she was on another mission, a different kind of treasure hunt.

At another rest stop Leah settled down on a graying apple tree. Breaking her thoughts from finding food on the ground was a loud crash and splintering of branches. Entering into the small clearing under the apple tree were two deer jumping out from among the dense thickets. One was a buck, large and powerful, its enormous antlers rivaling the stately look of a grand oak. Accompanying him was a much smaller slender doe. The buck held his head up, regal in its carriage, eyeing to the left then to the right for any danger as the doe commenced dining on the overly ripe fruit on the ground. As Leah watched with fascination, the buck reared up on his hind legs and retrieved a mouthful of the fresh fruit hanging from the higher branches. Standing taller now, his strong leg muscles bulged taut as they held his massive weight.

Leah noticed the great rack on his head. "He owns his own type of crown. It certainly brings out the royalty in him...quite like a king."

The impressive crown of antlers gave the buck a spirit of dignity, a sense that he was in control, a beast-king over an impressive territory; yet non-abusive nor overbearing. That was how Leah viewed the enigma she was following. His huge body and enormous wing span embodied power. But, it was those penetrating eyes, the ones she gazed into fleetingly before scrambling away in fear, that she sensed majesty, and in that majesty, control. But it was not the control that threatened, terrified, and destroyed. It was control with integrity. It was the kind of control of knowing whom he was that came through.

"I've witnessed it before, those uncontrolled, power-hungry beasts. Dogs chasing weaker animals for the mere thrill of the chase—to catch and destroy. Cats sneaking and crouching, waiting for their victim to wonder by. Worse still, it's usually without the real need for food, mercilessly teasing and playing with their victims before their cruel death."

As the deer finished their turn at the fruit buffet, they turned and scaled tall bushes back into the thickness of the forest. Their swift fluent moves bore graceful leaps, hanging in the air for fleeting seconds before disappearing.

Leah sighed as her eyes followed the tanned wonders. "They know who they are," she whispered. Then, as sadness came over her, she quivered, "Why don't I know who I am?"

She searched the area again looking for any slight movements, listening for any threatening sounds before she headed down. A tiny breeze stirred the broken end of a small limb dangling from a bush. A couple of white butterflies friskily sparred with each other in the air like a pair of snowflakes caught in an updraft. Two chipmunks clunked a constant Morse code back and forth, talking to each other through the verdant space. A dry leaf spun around crazily on the end of a barely visible spider's line.

Leah flew to the ground. Understandably, it was moist and mossy. The musty smell was thick with humidity as it covered the area like a damp blanket. Recent rains formed small puddles of water reflecting bits and pieces of sunlight through the thick barrier of leaves and branches. One puddle was just a few feet away from where Leah ate. She picked sparingly at the fruit, finding she was not as hungry as she had thought. The chase to catch the creature excited her, driving her to regard nothing else, not even food. Food was now more a chore than a joy. She went to the water for a drink. The deer hadn't disturbed it with their stomping.

"Hey! I haven't looked at myself in a long time." She bent over for a look in the watery mirror. "Who's that?" Leah turned around sharply, believing something menacing was behind her. But, nothing was there. She turned back to her reflection, her eyes growing wide with shock. "It's me!"

Leah turned her wings in and out slowly, appalled at her features that were in such terrible condition. She was flabbergasted that she could have flown so long without crashing to the ground. Feathers and tufts protruded everywhere along her body, nothing on her looked streamlined for quality maintained flying. Questions raced through her mind.

"How could things have gotten this bad?" she said. Leah turned her wings in and out in the reflection just as she did before to look at her newly-gained prized possessions. But this time it was a different story. "I can't believe this. With all the hard work I've done to look better, to feel better, with all the trouble I've gone through to get these feathers. The trouble to glue them on, all those close calls with death..."

That was it. Death; it was too close all the time. It didn't matter all the preparation that it had taken her or all the adversity that came against her, death's voice is what she heard mocking her, deriding her, laughing at her. It was death that played in her dreams, haunting her, keeping her from much needed sleep, never letting her rest. Rest. How she wished she could rest now; her mind, her body, and her emotions. But, to her it seemed a never-ending turmoil.

"Why didn't anyone tell me I looked like this?" Leah cried in anger. Immediately, images raced through her mind of the many that had tried to tell her: the Robin, the Chickadee, the Cardinal, the gentle Mourning Dove, and even the arrogant Seagull. Yet, the most important voice she heard, yet ignored, was her best friend Hoozer.

"I'm so sorry, Hoozer," Leah moaned. "I guess I just didn't want to hear anybody tell me anything. I just didn't want to hear at all." She forced herself to look one more time at her reflection and winced. She could not believe that all her plans were ruined, that nothing else she did could change any of it. "Oh, how I wish I could hear that giant bird's voice again. There's something about him that..."

But, instead, Leah heard a sound of another kind; crashing and breaking sound of ground brush directly behind her. In the instant she whirled around to see what was going on, she saw a rabbit careening wildly out of the thickets, zigzagging insanely toward her. The wild, crazed eyes of the frightened animal foretold something terrible. So quickly the rabbit came upon her that she had no time to think of escaping the inevitable collision. She tumbled over and over from the force, landing brusquely into a puddle. As fast as the rabbit had appeared it was gone, leaving her dazed, soaked, and covered with forest ground debris.

*What in the world happened?* Leah's thoughts were scattered. She was on her back, half submerged in the dirty water. Quickly, she scrambled in the muck trying to get out. It was the wrong move, for suddenly there was a second explosion of brush from the same direction the rabbit had emerged. But, it wasn't another rabbit running her way. This time it was one of the largest cats Leah had ever seen in her life. It was a Bobcat.

By the time she had stopped thrashing in the puddle it was too late. The wild cat had spotted her. The rabbit had been running for its life, the deadly threat directly behind it. Now Leah was between the rabbit and the cat. Now she was its target. The Bobcat stopped dead in its tracks. He had indeed spotted her. About twenty feet away from her, crouched low to the ground in its unmistakable feline stance, his great yellow eyes were hard secured on his new prey. Its paws dug ever so slightly into the soft ground for leverage, its leg muscles tight, readying its powerful forward leap.

Leah barely breathed. She could only stare back. Any movement would only mean a quicker death. She had no ideas, no plans for a getaway. A sharp pain rippled through her left wing shoulder. It was damaged from the impact with the rabbit, and there was nothing she could do about it. A bad wing was anathema to any bird. She was sure the Bobcat knew, or else he would have quickly charged to get an easy meal. Cats knew birds didn't stay on the ground long. This cat knew something was up and he was going to bide his time.

*How could I have been so stupid! Why didn't I just fly away when I heard the noise? That's what I'm supposed to do.* She stopped her derision as she watched the cat do something quite unexpectedly. Instead of the quick leap to end her life, he began a slow, deliberate creep toward her. He had already calculated her defenseless situation; he didn't need to hurry.

Leah was now even more horrified. She thought if this feline was anything at all like its domesticated cousins, the farm cats she's seen, the house cats she's known, then this one would probably do the same thing as they did: play cat and mouse with her before killing her. Leah knew this had to be the reason for his calculated moves toward her. If he were truly hungry he would have already been all over her.

Her thoughts then took a different twist, trying to erase the picture of the inevitable before her. A weight of magnitude proportions swept over her like a rain cloud bursting to release its contents over dry ground.

*When did all this start happening to me?*

This time an answer came to her. It was unexpected and it startled her. It came in a whisper from somewhere she could not even begin to imagine, a gentle yet firm answer; and she knew the answer to be true.

*'It started when you wanted to be someone you really weren't.'*

A crack of a twig brought Leah back to her morbid plight. The cat stopped short about fifteen feet from her, again hunched down, again waiting.

*What is he doing? Why doesn't he just get it over and done with?* Her mind screamed with fear and anger at the same time as the large cat continued eyeing her.

The cat was distracted by something overhead, which took his steely gaze off of her. He searched the treetops for a few seconds, scouring the green ceiling of the woods. Whatever it was that had captivated his attention was unseen, and his huge eyes traveled back down, once more boring deep into her spirit like daggers.

She was right. The wild cat had begun the cat and mouse game. Any slight move from her and the cat would take its cue and pounce on her, beginning the cruel game of death, ending only when the beast would decide he had had enough.

*What's the use? It's only a matter of seconds before my life is over.*

It was a very bizarre feeling; one that surprised her in the way it presented itself on this last stand she would be making. The wind rustled abruptly through the treetops. Without explanation, a great peace overwhelmed her just as it had when she was saved out of the pond and wrapped in a warm blanket of tranquility. It was a sublime quietude that filled her spirit back then after the harrowing ordeal. Now, from somewhere overhead, a mysterious invisible cloud came cascading down on top of her like hundreds of soft rose pedals falling in a gentle autumn wind. It left a gentle sweetness in the air filling her terrified and broken spirit. But was this real or was her imagination reeling with confusion due to the dreadful situation? Was this the peace before the storm? Whatever it was, Leah felt the release of pent up tension leave her body as every muscle relaxed despite the death-by-cat awaiting her only a few feet away. So, in the need to find hope, Leah forgot that to move would be the beginning of the end. She looked up toward the top of the trees.

Immediately, and instinctively, the cat made his move. Quickly turning her head back, Leah screeched in total horror as she watched the evil menace lunge toward her.

A second screech, one hundred times louder than hers, broke the atmosphere in a deafening boom, drowning out her frightened cries. Dropping out of the air, crashing down like a giant limb severed from a tree, a gigantic form descended upon both prey and enemy, shielding the hurt little bird from the cat's onslaught. In one quick moment Leah was encased in a large claw, held in like a prisoner surrounded by bars.

Another piercing cry from the dark apparition vibrated the atmosphere throughout the whole forest, fiercely rattling Leah's tiny body. An ensuing yelp responded in total fear. It was the terror-stricken cry of the wildcat. Leah could make out through the strong claws that the cat had come to a grinding halt a few short feet from her and her unlikely rescuer.

Like a powerful weapon, the huge bird opened its giant wings and flicked them at the stupefied cat, snapping at it with its dangerous beak narrowly missing the head. It only took seconds before Leah's shocked eyes, yet it all was surreal to her as though packed in an invisible grip of eternity. In those quick seconds, the cat retreated into the thickness of the forest without either meal of rabbit or bird. The tables were now turned. This time it was the cat's turn to run away in fear.

Leah was alive. But, there was something else she had to deal with now. There was no doubt in her that the large creature over her was the one she had been following, the one she had been trying to find. Its loud screech gave that away. But, now that she was in its claws and that it had as yet made no move to release her, Leah wondered if she was in an even worse predicament. There was no escaping these tremendous claws. They were as strong as iron bars, strong enough to hold anything and not let go.

# Chapter 14

# AQUILA

*But there is a friend who sticks closer than a brother.*
*- Proverbs 18:24*

L eah didn't know how long she had been underneath the creature. Everything was quiet now. It wasn't hard to guess that any slight move she made could force the gigantic claws to go into crush mode and it would be over instantly.

*What in the world was I thinking when I came to look for this… this…beast? Now it's got me! Who knows what it's going to do with me. Will it feed me to its own chicks? I wish it'd do something…anything! At least it would be all over with.*

She wished this same thing with the bobcat's maddening prey and enemy game. It took everything within her to even believe she could stay alive through that nightmare. Still in a quagmire of doubts, not knowing how long life would be extended, a gray mistiness enveloped her eyes blurring her vision. It came over her as gentle as the covering of the summer solstice after its long journey downward, as dusk paints the longest day done. Leah was barely aware what was going on around her. What little her eyes could make out did not make any sense. There was the ascent…up and up…over the tops of the trees…climbing and climbing, sailing through white, swollen clouds…entering the very blueness of the sky…elevating higher still as though surpassing the earth's atmosphere itself. There was nothing now but a silver illumination manifesting until finally…at last…they reached heaven.

A rough bump made Leah's eyes fly open. A loud gasp escaped her lips. For a few gripping seconds her mind went blank forgetting all that had happened. But harsh reality burst over her like ice water splashed onto her face. She wished she had never awakened because she was still a captive of the gigantic bird, still underneath it, and still in its clutches.

But, the next turn of events totally bewildered her. Very slowly the claw that incarcerated her began to release her. It lifted from around her, moving away ever so gently. Immediately, she became aware of the freedom when it let her go. A glimmer of hope came over her. She might still have a chance to escape. The monster could be caught off guard just as the fat bullfrog had been. If she could do it once, out-witting a carnivorous enemy, she could do it again. Yet, one problem remained— its massive bulk figure still towered over her. It hadn't moved away as she had hoped. With the imposing beak from this huge bird used against the Bobcat, it could easily seize her with lightning speed.

Leah believed that a little patience on her part might be the only tool to use until that blessed split-second surprise tactic would arrive. So for now, she concentrated on what was around her. Two legs huge as pillars and overlaid in feathers encased her on either side. The feathers were deepest brown with a slightly red-gold hue threaded throughout. The claws were enormous, wizened, and yellow. Its black talons were long and sharp, which could have torn the bobcat apart if it had wanted to.

*Is this the bird-thing I've been chasing? Why didn't I realize he was this big?*

There was something different about the terrain around her, different from the moist floor of the forest. She could sense it. She could smell it. The air was much cooler and drier. Gone were the humid, musty smells, the strong scent of pines that hung in the woods. Gone was the fruity aroma she smelled when she was feeding under the decayed apple tree. She was keenly aware that none of those things existed here. She couldn't smell aromatic floras, nor see any greenery typifying grasses. Curiosity now led the way past fear. Leah moved around to look from the confinement of the belly of the beast, careful to not make any sudden moves.

*Clouds!* She could not believe it. It was as though she could reach out and touch them. *Clouds this close, at eye level like this, can only mean one thing. I'm on a mountain!*

Leah whirled around. Behind her was a sheer wall of rock and ledges. She jerked to the right and saw an entrance that opened into a dark cave. She twisted back to the left and saw what she could only make out as the outside of what was probably her captor's nest; with detailed work of large limbs interwoven throughout with dried clumps of grasses, cattails, and bunched up leaves. Another wave of anxiety washed over Leah. She turned back again toward the clouds noticing that the ground, about fifteen feet in front of them, dropped off to nothing but thin air. Seeing the clouds in such close proximity had kept her from noticing they were on the ledge of a cliff. It was definitely a mountain. Leah had no trouble figuring out why this creature brought her to this remote high place.

*He's going to feed me to his brood! But, why me? I'm so little. I'm only a morsel to them. Why bring me this far when he could have easily eaten me himself?*

Yet, in all her confused and frightened notions, Leah could hear no noises indicating hungry chicks awaiting their dinner. She was on the ground, not in the nest. Throughout observing her surroundings, the giant bird had not made one single move to threaten her. She marked how one step either way could have ended it all for her.

"You can come out now, little one. It's safe."

Leah trembled uncontrollably. The voice scared her; there was no doubt about that. It wasn't the ear-piercing cry she's heard that could make one perish from shear fright. She just hadn't anticipated it talking to her at all.

"Don't be afraid, Leah Sparrow," the creature encouraged gently. "I won't hurt you."

Leah took in a sharp intake of breath. *He knows my name!*

"Come on out. Everything will be alright."

Not wanting to anger her captor, Leah replied with a quivering voice. "But, you'll eat me!"

The enormous voice chuckled heartily and answered, "I won't eat you. I'll feed you!"

*Feed me? What does he mean by that? I haven't been fed since I was a chick, and I can't possibly eat the same things he does, either.*

As though the creature had read her thoughts, he said, "I don't want to feed your body, Leah. I want to feed your heart."

Then, incredibly, the bird's remarkable head appeared under its left wing and peered intently at Leah. Once more they were face to face. Leah, who thought the one time encounter at the horse farm with those terrifying eyes was enough, was now staring right into them a second time. A pair of large golden orbs, hooded by strong furrowed brows, stared at her, and she could do nothing else but stare back. Instead of the ugly ravenous look of a hungry predator boring into her soul, these eyes held wonderment in them, a kind of joy that included her. Never had she met anything like this creature; she would have remembered. Whatever was happening between them was manifesting slowly, and slowly the terror in her heart began to subside. Involuntarily, she took a deep breath of cool fresh air from this huge bird's mountain on which she found herself. It felt good, as though her lungs had finally expanded after long constriction.

She noticed how close she was to the potent hooked beak that had nearly snapped off the bobcat's head. Undoubtedly it was a tool, a dangerous one, and now she was mere inches away from it. She studied the bird's crown feathers. A beautiful golden sheen flowed throughout the darker ones, like gold dusting brushed on them. Leah dared to imagine how magnificently the sun would bring out the shimmering glow of the feathers on this enigma of a bird.

She decided to make a move. Taking one careful step after another, she came out from under the mammoth figure. She could feel his eyes fixed on her every move; the hairs on her back stood on end. After a few steps, she slowly turned to face him. The creature straightened up, every hulking inch of him. Her bewildered eyes followed upwards along his great stature until she could take in the totality of his incredible physique. Although it was a striking picture of a predatory bird-beast, Leah could not miss how incredibly beautiful it was. A sense of majesty exuded throughout, taking her breath away.

"Who are you?" she asked, pulling her head far back and upwards so to fully take in his grand face.

"Hello, Leah!" he boomed with exuberance. "My name is Aquila. I am a Golden Eagle of the family Accipitridae, and my clan is the Aquila Chrysaetos. I am so glad to finally meet you." He lowered his magnificent head to her in a bowing manner. "I have been looking forward to this day for a very long time, little one."

Leah had heard about the Golden Eagles from her older clan members and other avifauna that lived close enough to the same terrain. *I've understood these great birds live by large bodies of water or high on the mountains. I've heard many tales about them, but I don't know what's true and what's myth. But, here I am, standing directly in front of one, staring at him, testifying to the fact that, yes, he is very real and very big. They will never believe me back home...if I live long enough to tell them.*

In a small trembling voice, Leah asked, "Are you saying that you know me?"

"Most assuredly!"

"But how?" Leah shot back. Immediately, she shrunk in fear not sure how this eagle would react to her inquisitiveness. But, she noticed a certain glimmer reflected in his huge eyes as though all the stars of the universe were held in them. "How do you know about me, Mr. Golden Eagle? I mean, we aren't from the same bird family. We don't live in the same territory. You don't go south for the winter like I do. Do you? So how can you know about me, and..."

"I don't know *about* you, Leah," the Golden Eagle interrupted, his smile shining. "I *know* you." He paused as though to let the answer sink in. "There's a lot of difference between the two, little sparrow. Knowing about someone is basically a list about them: what he does, where he goes, what he likes, what he dislikes, and so forth. But truly knowing someone is treasuring who he or she is because they are someone very special to you. It's the beauty of who they are on the inside, not what they are on the outside that we get to know."

Leah suddenly remembered about her appearance and about her new feathers. She lifted her wings to look at them and winced as a sharp pain shot through her. "Ow!"

"I'm so sorry you're hurt, Leah."

"It was my crash with the rabbit in the forest." Her face became hot with embarrassment. She had not preened herself since that fateful time. She could only imagine what she looked like. In all probability, a scary sight caked with dried mud, pieces of leaves, and cocky feathers sticking out all over her body. *What a mess I must be next to this magnificent bird. What could he possibly be thinking about me, the way I look?* Leah felt very close to bursting into tears.

With gentleness the Golden Eagle said, "Leah, never mind about the way you look. It's what's on the inside that matters. When you know who you are on the inside, you know who you are on the outside. That's what counts."

Leah raised her head in awe at the grand Eagle's ability to know what she had been thinking.

"Let me give you an example." The huge bird looked up toward the sky. "The sun is big and hot, right?"

"Yes."

"Clouds—those dark, stormy ones, or the thick white ones, or even skies that are just gray and overcast—when they cover the sun, does the sun stay the same or does it change into something else behind those clouds?"

"It stays the same."

"Right. Now, we might not be able to see it clearly, and we might not be able to feel its full affects, but nothing stops the sun from *being* the sun. It can't stop *being* who it is." The eagle took his eyes off of Leah and focused far away into nothingness as the once close clouds Leah almost breathed in had moved away from the mountain. The sky was a glorious cobalt blue as far as the eye could see. "Now, little sparrow, answer me this. No one can look straight at the sun for a very long time, right?"

"Right."

"That's because the sun is that powerful in who it is; its radiance, its splendor. No matter what covers it, what gloom comes over it, what storm rages against it, the sun is still bright, still shining, and still strong behind it all. It is who it is on the inside. It is what it was created to be."

Leah was amazed. The eagle expressed himself with strong conviction. His wisdom flowed smoothly and refreshingly into her very core as though a barren, desert wasteland had finally turned into a fruitful oasis. An incredible theory formed in Leah's mind.

"You were the one that saved me that first time when I almost crashed into the pond in my woods, weren't you?" she asked. She remembered the flash of something big and shadowy beside her that helped glide her to safety.

The Golden Eagle smiled.

"And you were the one who saved me from Shadow at the horse farm, too, weren't you?"

Again, the huge bird did not answer, but kept his eyes on her as though she was the most important thing in the world to him. He was giving her his full attention.

"And, just now, you saved me from that wild cat in the big forest." It wasn't a question now because Leah knew. She was certain of the one who had been there for her. But there was something else she desperately needed answered. "But, how did you know...how could you have known…when I was in trouble? I should have been dead many times over!"

The Golden Eagle looked piercingly at Leah and said, "Sweet Leah, I want to save more than your body. I want to save *you*. Save who you are."

"Save who I am? What do you mean?" Leah asked, still uncertain as to why this great bird was even subjecting himself to someone so unworthy as she was.

"Leah, I have seen you since the day you came back in the spring, when you began feeling miserable about being small, about being drab, as you said, and not liking yourself very much."

Leah's breath caught in her throat at the very word of disgust she had spit out about herself when she first returned from her winter home. This Eagle once again showed that he knew something else about her; more than anyone ever did.

"I know about the day you found your first new feather and how you attached it. I know about the struggles in acquiring them all. I've also seen the natural enemies nearly destroy you in the process." He paused. "But, worst of all, Leah, I've seen another enemy trying to take control of you, and it has tried to destroy you for a very long time."

Leah stared in stunned silence as she waited for the Eagle to continue. *How could he even notice, let alone care for, such a small thing like me? I'm such an insignificant speck of a bird compared to him.*

"That's what I mean, Leah. You look at yourself in the wrong light, in the worst way."

He answered her very thoughts, again. But, before she could say anything, the Golden Eagle moved to the edge of the cliff. He looked out into the deep, green valley below them. The opulent shield of trees blanketed most of the valley for miles, yet some areas opened into succulent meadows not easily spotted by normal eyes. It made wonderful grazing land for forest animals. Like the deer. The eagle's keen eyesight had spotted them.

"Come over here, Leah. I want to show you something."

She couldn't believe her ears. At this height she was afraid to go anywhere near the edge of the mountain. Her wing was damaged. She was sure she would easily be swept off to her death by the strong winds. She didn't budge.

"It'll be alright," he encouraged. "The winds, though treacherous at times, are pretty quiet right now."

Leah still didn't move.

Then the Eagle looked squarely into her face and said, "I'll watch over you, Leah. I promise."

He was telling the truth. Why would he fail her now when he had been there for her many times before? His voice held such sincerity that it brought a calming effect over her. She moved to the edge along beside him and braved a look over the land far below. It was a stunning view. Never had she been so far up into the sky and still be on solid ground. Had the clouds remained close to them she could have felt them on her face. Her species depended on the low ground for seed and water, for insects and berries, and other things to maintain their existence. They were dependent on trees and bushes, even buildings for nest homes. And although they traveled far and wide to their winter homes, there was never really any need to travel to such high mountainous altitudes.

"We must be at the edge of the world," Leah whispered. She looked southwest toward her region. "Will I ever see my nest home again?" A homesick feeling settled in the deepest part of her being.

"You'll see greater things than these, Leah," the Eagle said softly.

She turned her head to look up at the remarkable figure, then out over the ledge, and back to the Golden Eagle again. He was staring out farther past anything Leah knew she could see. He had his strange ways of knowing her very thoughts, and that was intriguing in itself, but it quite amused her that he would declare she would see even more than what had already passed before her stunned eyes since their outlandish meeting. Her mind couldn't digest it all.

*I'm going to see more? But, look at what I'm seeing now: a remarkable Golden Eagle that certainly none of my own clan and species has ever encountered. To top it off, I'm still alive and standing on top of a huge mountain with clouds that practically touch my head. What else can I possibly see?*

The Golden Eagle answered again in his uncanny way. "I want you to focus, Leah, and I'll show you what you'll see. Out there, by that small clearing in the trees where the sun's rays are piercing through the clouds. Do you see anything?"

Leah peered hard toward where he was describing, but all she could see was the same thing over and over—rich dark vegetation of the lush forest.

"Focus, Leah," he stressed again. "Don't look at what you can see. Concentrate on what you can't see."

"What?"

She was confused now, but the Eagle didn't answer her, so she did as she was told. She focused harder, her eyes scanning the tops of the trees, back and forth, to the point of exasperation. She was angry with herself that she couldn't do what was asked of her. But she persevered and, finally, a lighter patch of emerald-green displayed itself in the umbra sea of trees. Two tiny figures appeared into her view in the open space. Leah was overjoyed at her find.

"I see a meadow! I can see two figures there now, but I can't tell what they are."

"Good, girl!" the Eagle encouraged. "You're right. That's a meadow and those two figures are deer—a doe and a buck."

Slightly startled, Leah said, "I wonder if they're the ones I saw earlier today feeding under the fruit tree. The buck was an awesome fellow. I remember seeing his exceptional strength when he stretched up for the fruit on the tree."

"Would you have known they were deer if I wouldn't have told you?"

"Well, no. I couldn't really see them clearly."

"Exactly. You couldn't see them with your natural eyes, but when I told you who they were you recognized them with your inner eyes."

Leah cocked her head to the side as if to help her understand what he was saying. "With my what eyes?"

"From this perspective the deer are small and insignificant looking, but in reality we both know they are noble creatures of the woods and the meadows. They're not small and they're not insignificant." The Golden Eagle could tell by Leah's small frown on her face that she was concentrating on what he was saying. "So, we know that if we were close to them they would look totally different. You know that the buck, with his impressive antlers, is not something to be trifled with. We know that when he stomps his hoof he means business and wants attention. We know that two bucks will fight greatly for their territory. The mother doe will lift her white tail high in the air to warn her fawns when there's danger around. Up close we know who they really are."

Leah kept looking at the two tiny dots as she listened attentively to the eagle. Then, staring even farther away than Leah knew she could see, past the mountainous horizon into another unseen world, the Eagle spoke. "When we are close and in perspective to that which we really are, we are truly seeing ourselves with our inner eyes, Leah. Those inner eyes are our *good* eyes." He turned to face her.

"Our good eyes?" A dazed look crossed her face like shade moving under a tree.

"Yes. What we see with our natural eyes we immediately perceive with our mind and readily judge it, and most often than not, we judge things wrongly. But, with the inner eyes, our good eyes, we see more clearly, more truthfully. You formed the image of the deer with your inner eyes before you could really see them with your physical eyes, and then you saw them, the true them."

The Eagle looked at Leah with his intense golden eyes. She sensed deep within that he was reading her even then by what he had been talking about—with his good eyes. The deep fear she had been so accustomed to, like a coat of armor, slowly began to fall away. Little by little, she began to relax as the anxiety all over her body evaporated like the morning mist.

"When we look at ourselves with good eyes, Leah, we become strong in who we really are and who we were always meant to be."

Suddenly, an immense gust of wind pounded against the side of the mountain and, with great force, surged up its side. In an instant, the Eagle thrust out his huge wing and guarded Leah from its onslaught. He braced against its intensity by lowering closer to the ground. Leah lowered her head against the sturdiness of his long pinions. The powerful feathers that carried him, and at times fought for him against ferocious open skies, were now protecting her against the untamed gale. It stopped as abruptly as it had come. They both straightened up and ruffled their feathers, shaking off the dust that had been stirred up around them.

"Well, it's time," the Eagle whispered mysteriously. But, then, with firmness, he added, "Leah, go back from the ledge now and stand by the mouth of the cave."

Leah shook with apprehension again. She didn't know what was going on.

With gentleness, the giant bird said, "It'll be alright. The cave is safe. I go in there myself when it's necessary."

Leah did as he requested, curious now as to why she had to move back and away from him.

"I have to go away for a short time, little one."

"What?" Leah squealed. A worried look enveloped her face. "You're going to leave me?"

"I promise you I'll be back. Stay close to the cave. The winds shift quite suddenly as you've seen, and they're too strong for you." With a pained look he glanced at her wing. "Remember your wing, Leah. I'm sorry you're hurt, but that's why I want you farther back." He looked at her again. He could see her great concern. He emphasized once more with strong sincerity in his voice, "I will be back."

Leah could detect the truest form of sincerity in his voice for her to believe him.

"Yes, Mr. Golden Eagle, I…"

"No, no. It's Aquila. Just call me Aquila."

"Yes, Mister…I mean…Aquila. I'll be waiting for you," Leah responded softly. But Leah was only saying a half-truth. She would wait for him, but she wasn't quite sure she was ready to say she could fully trust him. Not yet. It had only been a few hours since her almost disastrous flight chasing him, fewer still being in his presence. It surprised her how things had turned out, but it would take more time for her to trust this mystery of a bird all the way.

*Aquila. Hmm...even his name has a lordly ring to it. But, of course, it would have to, to truly describe something as extraordinary as he is.* Leah went toward the cave. *But what is he up to?* She turned around in time to see Aquila facing outward at the very edge of the cliff, his wings spread out. Her eyes bulged out in shock at their enormous size. *They must be as wide tip to tip as a horse is front to back. They spread out forever!*

As he stood in front of her, she sensed a fearless spirit surging from him as though he was a special guardian on top of the world, watching, catching something amiss so he could intervene. Leah could easily believe that. The eagle's copper sheen streaked through the darker ones in the brightness of the sun's rays, shining like gold veins in a deep mine.

*No wonder he's called a Golden Eagle. I wonder if he could carry a hundred of us sparrows on his back and wings.*

An explosion of wind came and hit Aquila squarely, lifting some of the larger feathers from his body. It was the perfect volley he wanted. Balancing himself with his massive wings, he became air-borne, smoothly gliding out over the ledge. Quickly, he shifted back and forth as the wind blew fiercely. His tail fanned out for balance like a paddle in water. Holding steady on the wind, he looked downward, searching the world through resolute eyes. Aquila clung to the under draft as he glanced one last time toward Leah.

Leah watched as the Golden Eagle rode the current and sailed out into the open sky. He was floating and shifting, a dance in the wind, as he went farther away from the mountain and from her. She resisted the urge to run to the ledge to watch him before he disappeared from sight, but she knew better. She needed to heed what he said. Being swept off the mountain by a strong wind and tossed around like a loose feather tuft would be sure death.

"What tremendous strength he has," she whispered. "If it was me in that current I'd already be on a peak of the next mountain!"

Suddenly, a horrific screech echoed through the atmosphere, ricocheting off the barriers of the mountains, and diminishing to earth in an invisible wave. Aquila was gone. Leah was awestruck at the spectacular sight. In the one hand, he was like a melody in flight. On the other, he was the epitome of terror with natural menacing looks and an awesome form of power. Nobody could deny acknowledging that he was a king of the sky and maybe even of the whole animal world. At least, Leah's known world. She was disappointed that she was alone, but she reassured herself with the words Aquila told her, "I will be back."

"I wonder where he went." She gazed into the azure sky. Aquila was nowhere in sight. The sun continued its brilliant gleam. Leah could see white streaks blazing across the open air from the human's flying machines as they flew overhead. Drifting peacefully, white elongated clouds made a stream toward the west. She turned away from the ledge.

*Well, what am I going to do while he's gone?* She let out a short impatient sigh.

She strolled around the wide cliff to inspect the area. The rock wall went another thirty feet straight up the mountain, protruding rock formations appearing intermittently. To her left was the huge nest. It was a sturdy nest built to hold large birds.

"I need to investigate things around this strange mountain, and I think I'm going to start with the cave." Stepping out from under the sunshine, she cautiously stepped into the cave. Although Aquila had told her that he himself went into it, she was leery about entering someplace she was not used to. Leah slowly adjusted to the dark and immediately noticed a peculiar thing. Strewn around the floor of the cave were feathers, lots of them. She could only think of one logical explanation about this Aquila Chrysaetos.

"Boy, he must molt a lot."

The absence of the sun along with the help of the mountain's rock walls kept the cave's temperature low inside. A cool stiffness permeated throughout. There were small fissures in the walls around the cave, indentations that looked like little nests. Small boulders were scattered about the floor and it was there that Leah spotted bits of dried bone lying on the floor next to them. She didn't want to think too hard about what these findings could mean. She turned back to the cave's opening.

Leah paced back and forth impatiently at the mouth of the cave waiting for Aquila to return. She periodically looked at the sky searching for a dark figure hanging close to the mountain. From a far distance toward the west Leah perceived the distant sound of a flock of geese. Their silhouetted streamlined flight against the sun reminded her of that first day of spring after she returned to her summer homeland. She also remembered how she did not want to be who she was.

*I guess I'm feeling better because of the good things Aquila has been speaking to me.* Her shoulders sagged; drooping wing tips almost touched the ground. *But, then, I'm up here on this mountain and not down there on the ground where life is so different.*

The mountains held Leah in awe. She had seen them enough times before, though only from a far distance. Light gray clouds converged onto the peaks making the mountains appear shorter in their loftiness then they really were; moody monuments, exalted parts of earth with fewer life forms and fiercer winds then its lower counterparts.

"I wonder how long Aquila's kind has lived up here? As long as the mountains are old? He seems so ancient to me, like he's always existed. I can see it in his eyes, so wise, so full of thought from long ago." Her own thoughts went back to the feathers that were scattered inside the cave. An idea flashed across her mind. "Aquila's feathers. I need to take a closer look at them out here in the sunlight. They're magnificent, not like any others I've ever seen."

That same urge she had since spring and throughout the summer welled up inside of her again. It was a deep-seeded urgency for something more, something else to help her better understand who she was. And like a flash of lightening from the east to the west, the realization came that what she wanted more than anything else was to be like Aquila. She had to see one of his feathers.

"Wait a minute. What if Aquila comes back and sees me with it?" Leah stopped abruptly. "What if he gets mad? What would he do to me? I still don't know him very well."

Yet the questions and the trepidation she felt were promptly obscured by her insatiable curiosity. The desire to avail her of an eagle feather was a great one. She continued forward and stepped once again into the dismal cave. Before she went farther, she glanced back to the bright opening to see if the Golden Eagle had returned. Detecting nothing, she went ahead.

This time, as she inched toward the area where she had seen the feathers, she felt as though she was walking on sacred ground, that something of great significance happened there. She didn't think it was a feeding ground at all, but an area of some ancient rite, solemn and important. Leah didn't understand how she knew this, but she felt an impression that this was so. She quickly picked up a feather and hurried out.

Just by the way the feather lay across her small frame and head, Leah had retrieved a rather superior feather. She stopped at the cave's opening to avoid any surprise winds buffeting the mountain at the cliff's edge. Laying the feather down on the ground, she placed her foot over its quill tip. It was definitely Aquila's feather. It had that same deep reddish-brown color with the unmistakable golden threads glittering throughout as the sun's rays flitted against it. But, this feather looked old, well used. The quill was brittle with a slightly grayish coloring, the tip broken and jagged. The thin individual hairs were scraggily, ragged in some sections as though worn out. By its size and color Leah could see that this was once a main pinion of his wing.

"But there are so many feathers on the floor of the cave. Are they all Aquila's?"

She knew all birds molted, but she was surprised as to how many feathers she had seen. Now, she was more curious about this strange bird than ever before. Finishing inspecting the feather, Leah worried that Aquila would catch her with it and disapprove. As soon as she removed her foot off the feather, a sudden gust of wind rushed up over the ledge faster than she could react. The feather dashed up the rock wall making loop-the-loops, over and over, and sailed away from the mountainside; away from its hold and out into the spacious blue sky. It was gone in seconds. Leah knew there was nothing she could do. What she did do was watch the feather flounce about until it was swallowed in the folds of some far away clouds.

"Wow. That was fast. I wonder where that feather will end up out there in that great, big world," she whispered, her heart pounding, longing to fly again. "That odious bobcat robbed me of my very existence. But, I'll be out there soon. I hope."

A tremendous swooshing noise broke through her musing. With a thudding heart, she quickly twirled around to find Aquila coming in for a landing. His giant wings stirred dust and pebbles as he gracefully maneuvered downward. Leah scooted deeper into the cave to escape being blown over as he landed. She saw that Aquila had not come back empty-handed. He held something in each of his powerful claws. One held the remains of a huge fish, no doubt his dinner. The other item was a branch filled with sweet berries, the kind that Leah had been eating before the wildcat's attack. She only now remembered how hungry she was.

Aquila spoke first. "I brought you something to eat, Leah. I hope you like these berries." He laid them down in front of her.

"Yes, I do. Thank you, Mister…I mean, Aquila." Leah wondered how he could have known she liked these particular types of berries. But then, of course, he was different, so knowing, she could almost believe anything about him now.

He walked just short of the mouth of the cave and deposited his catch onto the ground. "I know seeing this creature repulses you, but I do need to eat," Aquila said gently, but without apology.

"Yes, of course, you do. I understand," she replied, grateful that she didn't have to eat fish.

"It's getting late, little one," he said, as mysteriously now as he was before leaving. "It'll be dark very soon."

Heaving a quiet sigh, he stared toward the darkening west. The mountains cast their long shadows over the expanse of the tree land. It saddened Leah as she watched the beauty of the valley covered in a deep umbra. She also noted a sad and tired manner in the way Aquila said "very soon." But she didn't ask him any questions.

The winds had spent themselves to a standstill, but not before dispersing the clouds for the moon's full face to glow in the night. The moon's lucent beam shone all over the land below them, casting its mellow silvery hue onto the earth.

*I wonder what's on his mind. It's obvious he's not taking me back down the mountain today. I'm pretty vulnerable with a bad wing, but Aquila has been nothing but gentle and kind toward me the whole time. He has even kept his word that he would feed me, and he brought me some berries.* She had not understood the true meaning of what Aquila meant as she pecked at a few berries. The excitement of all that had transpired in the short time with him had diverted any pangs of hunger until now.

"Leah." Aquila moved to the cave's opening where she stood. With the moonlight's gleam shining behind him she could see how intimidating he could be, giving him an ominous look, a larger-than-life appearance. "Leah, it's time to feed you."

"But, I'm already eating!" she quipped, glancing at her berries, wondering why he didn't catch on. Aquila gave a hearty laugh. Leah joined in, though not sure what was so funny.

"Leah, remember when I told you to come out so I could talk to you? That I was going to feed you?"

She nodded.

"Well, I also told you that it was not physical food I was talking about. There is a kind of food that we all need that is just as important for us as the physical food. This other kind of food nourishes our inner self." Aquila looked up into the night, so elegantly studded with millions of stars. He took a deep breath of air as though he was drinking in the very essence of the glorious lights into himself. "When we drink in the beauty around us, Leah, we feel as though we are a part of it. But to breathe in that beauty around us every day we must first acknowledge that it exists. We must realize that it exists for the purpose of feeding us its very own strength through our senses: our eyes, our sense of smell, our hearing, and so forth, but, most importantly, feeding our spirit."

Aquila stopped talking. A few seconds passed. He cocked his head slightly to one side. "Listen, Leah."

Leah mimicked Aquila, also leaning her head to one side. "What can I possibly hear way up hear on this mountain? There's nothing up here. But where I'm from nothing seems to sleep. Not the peepers, certainly not the frogs…oh, and definitely not the crickets. Sometimes I can hear dogs barking far away and the human's cars, too. Who can hear anything above all that racket?"

"Concentrate, Leah!" Aquila said strongly. Then, in a more gentle tone, he said, "Now, listen, but not only with your ears."

*Okay. Now he's talking weird.* Rolling her eyes, Leah adjusted her thinking as Aquila told her. Her heart was only just beginning to calm down after the attacks on her life. It's expected in the animal kingdom; nature was not always kind to the weaker creatures. But the hope that it could be avoided was ever present. Standing on top of the high-peaked mountain with a hurt wing and with her mind reeling from the pain of wondering what her purpose in life was, she found herself desperately wishing she could hear the answers. *Quiet!* Leah scolded herself. *I have to stop thinking about everything. Stop thinking, Leah!* It was not going to be easy. Scenes tumbled across her mind like clouds in a tempest.

Aquila had been still for a long time. Leah sneaked a peek at him as she fidgeted around. *Did he fall asleep? I guess I've got to focus harder by doing what Aquila's doing. Close my eyes, too, and relax.* Stillness slowly came through concentration. After a few moments she was mildly surprised how calm she did feel. A sensation slowly drifted over her as she noticed the muffled sound of distant thunder echoing from a faraway summer storm.

*Hmm…how different that rumbling sounds at a far distance than when it booms and crashes right overhead. It almost sounds inspiring.*

*What a difference perspective makes.* Leah remembered what Aquila had taught her earlier. *If that storm was looming overhead it would have pierced my eardrums with all its clamoring. It would have been useless to try to rest through that.*

Once more she fixed on being still as the thunder faded. Then there was something else. The evening breeze began moving with more energy. It wasn't the full force gale as earlier in the day, but a smooth measure that floated across the mountain's face. This confluence carried soft whistling sounds into space as it swept across gaps and ridges, high and low peaks, playing across them like stringed instruments. Nature was playing her evening song. Leah lifted her face toward the night sky as though to allow the discovered music envelop her.

She was overjoyed by the find. She had never heard sounds quite like this, never expecting that it could come from high on the mountains. She's been aware of the beautiful voice of the Yellow Warbler and other birds with better songs than hers. That's why she had desperately wanted their feathers; a part of them to be like them. But, even that did not compare to the floating melody she was now hearing. Restfulness came over her as though she was enfolded in a billow of clouds, as comfortable to her as the feathered mother-arms cradling her when she was a little bird safe in her nest home.

# Chapter 15

# A MOUNTAINOUS CHANGE

*Earth changes, but thy soul and God stand sure.*
*–Robert Browning*

L eah heard faint knocking sounds coming from behind her. She quickly looked around. Aquila was gone. Shocked that she was unaware when he moved, (it should have been fairly easy to hear his lumbering moves) she glanced toward the direction of the cave to see if he was there.

*Boy, I must have really been lost in quietness. That's a first. But where in the world is Aquila? He was standing right here beside me. Why did he leave me? He should know this place is too scary for me to be alone.*

Again the rapping sounded. She was certain it was coming from inside the cave. She quietly went to investigate. The full moon radiated enough to beam some sort of light inside. She quickly detected something was terribly wrong. Stepping toward a boulder, she could sense Aquila's presence in the dark. She heard heavy calculated breathing.

"Aquila?"

"Don't come any closer."

Leah stopped, surprised by the abrupt command. Aquila sounded very strange. She quickly noticed that he didn't say her name when he spoke. Early on, she had the distinct impression he enjoyed letting her know how important she was to him and it had made her feel special. But now her feelings were hurt. He told her he didn't want her near him. But, she couldn't just leave. Not yet. She had questions rising up in her faster than the abrupt winds she had experienced in this foreign place.

"Aquila, what's going on?" Leah whispered. Fear forced its way into her voice. She swallowed hard. "What's wrong?" There was no answer. "What's the matter, Aquila? Are you sick? Can I help you?" Anxiety rose as the day's temperature at every question she asked. She wanted answers, but none came. "Aquila, I don't understand. Why won't you tell me what's going on?" In desperation, she slowly started toward Aquila again, hoping he would not object this time.

"No!"

Leah's throat caught in a small stifled cry. She was startled by his impatient response. All she wanted to do was help. Aquila seemed to sense her apprehension because his tone changed.

"Stay where...you are. You can't help me. Go, now, and rest."

A weak, tortured moan reached Leah's ears from behind the rock, her concern escalating even more. Unable to comprehend why he wouldn't let her do something for him, anything, she kept her distance. He had plainly told her he didn't want her help. Her shoulders sunk.

"OK, Aquila. If that's what you want, I'll leave you alone." She turned to the right side of the cave, away from the unpredictable bird so as not to disturb him. "Good night."

There were no more words from the Golden Eagle; no more words of comfort from him spiriting to her since coming to his mountain. Leah settled in the farthest end of the cave in a small crevice. For certain, Aquila was not himself. Mystified and upset, all she could really do was trust him. She had to. But, she knew the battle through the night would be the disturbing questions in the cave of her mind that twisted and turned continuously, a tortuous tunnel bearing no answers. Whatever was happening to him was going to be revealed in the morning. She just had to wait the night out as patiently as she could, but she knew it was going to be a very long and painful wait. As she closed her eyes, shivering with dread and frustration, she knew patience was not her greatest virtue.

The next day came cascading its golden sheen over the mountains. But the cave faced to the west and was still cloaked in a shadowy haze. Leah felt about as much in a haze as the day had begun. Yet, she found that she had slept most of the night even after the strange episode with Aquila. She accredited it all to the fact that she had a very high-geared and trying day yesterday. The long flight to find Aquila, followed by the narrow escape from the bobcat, and ending with the final miraculous encounter with her new friend, that although dangerous and exciting at the same time, it all brought along with it its natural exhausting uncertainty.

Patiently, Leah waited for Aquila to make his first move. She didn't want to upset him again. Strange scratching and scraping sounded throughout the night and thoughts of little mice came to mind as she pictured them scurrying around the cave, possibly digging a hole for them. But, Leah was sure Aquila would not allow mice to infiltrate his domain because they were food; they wouldn't last long. Then everything finally grew quiet.

The day grew brighter scattering the last wisps of the ashen shade from the mountain. Light pierced the cave's gloominess. She glanced toward the spot where she last sensed Aquila's presence.

"He's gone!" Leah scrambled to the boulder where more feathers were scattered on the floor than what she had seen yesterday. Feathers trailed out of the cave and out into the open. "What on earth happened?" Leah's face contorted in total shock. Her heart was at her throat. An agonizing fear hit the pit of her stomach. Again, Aquila had left during the night without Leah being aware of it. She had no idea where he had gone. "What's happening? It looks terrible here, like…like…" Leah let out a loud gasp. "Like as if some beast got to him last night. Maybe that's what happened. Maybe that's why so many feathers are all over the place." Intense fear twisted Leah's stomach into knots. She stopped as a horrifying prospect entered her mind. "Now what am I going to do? What am I going to do here…without Aquila?"

Assessing the cruel situation she seemed to be facing, thoughts of an immediate escape came to her mind. "What if a large carnivorous animal killed him? It could be waiting just outside the cave. I am not going to remain and be prey to whatever destroyed my new friend, hurt wing or not." Like a flash, an idea emerged. "I'll make a furious dash out of the cave here; throw myself over the ledge, and quickly free-fall downward. I hope there's no turbulence so that I can float safely down to the forest below. Even with my wing still hurting, I could dash about quicker than any cumbersome creature waiting outside for me. A creature that could come and take out Aquila has to be an enormous predator. This is my only hope." With terror raging inside, Leah said, "But what could be larger and stronger up here than Aquila?"

She braced herself for the worst. As she plunged ahead with all the courage she could gather, she burst into the sunlight and onto the ledge. Squinting from the brightness, it came to her how ironic it was that the day could be filled with such radiant sunshine even as tragic as the day had begun. She ran as though ghosts were chasing her. But, just as quickly, she came to a complete stop, for right in front of her was a large dark hulk on the ground, unmoving. Her worst fears had become reality.

"No-o-o!" Leah screamed.

It was Aquila. Leah didn't breathe. She couldn't.

As the universe still continued around her—a tiny whistling note from the wind playing past a dried bush, the faraway echoing hum of the human's airship, the beat of loose falling rocks—Leah heard something else that made her heart skip a beat; the intake of massive breath. She waited again, her wings covering a tormented cry trying to escape, her eyes bulging out and brimming with tears. Then it came, the release of breath that moved the body slightly. Finally, Leah could release her own breath and tears flowed freely.

Distraught by the whole scene, she now saw her friend not as the giant, majestic bird she had come to know only yesterday. Before her now was a heap of ragged torn feathers, mottled with dirt and bits of twigs and gravel. His legs were extended out from under his body, but his claws were curled inward. The powerful talons were broken and jagged; unfit tools for a bird of prey.

"What happened to him? Who did this to him?" Leah cried in a whisper. She didn't want to believe what she was seeing. Slowly, she went around Aquila's once beautiful head, dirty and disheveled, when a more piteous sight met her as she stepped in front of him. The tip of his immense beak was a broken mess. *He's not going to make it!* Leah's heart broke into a million pieces. *He'll never survive out here even if he lives past this brutality.* Bending over to look closely at her once powerful friend, Leah cried softly, "Oh, Aquila, what happened to you?"

All of a sudden, Aquila's eyes flew open and caught her by surprise. She quickly drew back. As he fixed his gaze on her, she detected great pain behind the huge globes. Yet, she could also see the same gentle concern he had shown her from the beginning.

"Don't worry. I...I'll...be all right." He took a deep breath, "No one...did this...to me."

Aquila closed his eyes again as though he were going to sleep. Leah had caught a glimpse of the same Aquila even behind the pain, the Aquila that was inside, the strong wise Aquila. But, she still worried. Will he ever be the same again on the outside? That endowment of beauty, power, and bravery that made him what he was?

*Will he be able to fly again, or catch his prey, or even be able to eat it? His body is so broken!* She stood by Aquila like a guard beside his king. That is what he had become to her, something of nobility and wonder, one due fearful respect. She had come to value the fear of that presence in him, not a frightening fear, but a reverent fear. It was demonstrated in his walk, in his speech, in his appearance; it exuded out of him. He wore it like a royal crown, though he did not demand it, he did not abuse it. He lived it.

It was his show of deep concern for her, one of the smallest avifauna, that made Leah realize he was so different, so unlike all the others, that she wondered if he was from this world. Even with his massive size, his awesome feathers and wing span, even with his tremendously powerful claws and terrifying beak, Aquila's heart beat for those weaker than he. He pursued her during her weakest times, during the most perilous times in her life. He pursued her, Leah Sparrow, like no one else ever had.

*But look at him now.* Leah stared hard at the weakened Golden Eagle. She was taken by surprise as a strange thought popped into her mind. *He's...ugly.*

She was miserable. Lying on the ground between the ledge and the cave, the hot sun beating its relentless rays on his crumpled body, Aquila was vulnerable and open prey to anything stronger than him now. Her thoughts led her to the worst things imaginable that could happen to him. Then, another feeling crept up inside her that caught her off guard. She was angry, angry that he was not able to be with her any more like at the start. She was surprised how quickly she had gotten used to it—the idea of depending on him for strength and help. She got used to how he could scatter frightening things, seen or unseen, away from her. How he called out her name, how his total attention was toward her as tough they were the only two creatures in the world.

Aquila rested under the blanket of heat, basking under unseen healing properties that streamed down onto his hurting torso and spirit. The same heat was helping curb Leah's shivering body, chilled from all the anxious moments since she had awakened and discovered Aquila. She was grateful for the sun.

Quite unexpectedly, a large shadow floated over both of them. Leah quickly turned her head up to search the sky. She saw a large, black apparition against the blueness of the sky as it circled wide. It was clear to her that the creature was investigating the poor condition of a hurt animal. The intruder had undoubtedly scented Aquila's weakened state. It came around again, lower this time, for a closer look. She was sure it was a scavenger bird, and they were not particular to what they ate as long as it was dead. Leah knew she had no power to control, let alone stop any attack on Aquila should the intruder decide to do so.

*Aquila will be no match for an attack, and neither will I.* Still, as Leah continued watching the figure overhead, she inched closer and closer to Aquila, leaning into him, not for protection, but to protect. "I don't know what I can do, but I'll do whatever it takes to keep him safe. I don't care how small I am, I am not about to let anything take advantage of my friend's horrible state, not while I'm around."

Her small body shivered with excitement as her mind raced with wild thoughts of what she could do to help Aquila in the worse-case scenario, regardless what was flying above them. She tried to stay ahead of the fear that was mounting inside. But, as she watched, the intruder began to circle away from them, higher and farther until it was totally out of sight.

"Whew! That was too close." Leah breathed a sigh of relief, thankful that nothing happened. "I'll have to keep watching should it decide to return. I'm certain it was sizing up the situation here on the cliff. But what will it do the next time if it decides to come back?"

Leah turned back toward Aquila and was startled. Aquila was staring at her. She detected a genuine glint of gratitude in his eyes.

"Thank you," he squeezed out. "Thank you...for thinking... about me."

Leah didn't really know what to say. Even in his pain and suffering, Leah found it incredible that he still endeavored to thank her for what little she did for him. Suddenly, she felt ashamed, not wanting to look into his eyes. She remembered her earlier thoughts of how she felt abandoned and alone and that she would have to fend for herself.

*It wasn't even his fault. How selfish can I be? I'm always thinking about myself and my needs.* She paused. She shook her head in misery. *It's always been about me.*

But she didn't have any time for further self-abasement as she noticed Aquila begin to move. He proceeded to turn over onto his opposite side. With great difficulty and without a word, he settled back down again, this time soaking in the full strength of the sun's heat waves on his opposite side.

*I'm glad today's a sunny day. Hopefully it'll help Aquila feel better. I mean, even I can tell the difference flying in sunny days as compared to gloomy ones. Nobody likes dark days around them, dark clouds... over...them.* Leah's thoughts trailed off. What she was reasoning rang through her loud and clear as clanging bells from fish boats offshore at the Big Waters; loud and noisome, reminding everyone that they were there. *That's exactly where I've been living in for a long time now, under dark, gloomy clouds. But it's all been my own doing.* She paused, letting out a tiny whimper. *Yes, I've fought hard for these feathers, feathers that represent everything I want to be. But now I'm not sure if it's all been for nothing. I feel so lost, so opposite of what I wanted for myself.*

Leah took an extensive look at her out-stretched wings, and although somewhat rumpled, the multicolored feathers were still intact. She lifted her head, rolling her eyes back as far as she could. Suddenly feeling silly thinking she could see whether her Cardinal tuft was on top of her head, she let out a grunt of exasperation.

Without warning, in the tempo of a millisecond, she felt the odd sensation of being yanked up and away from the ground, with the bizarre thought that her spirit was being detached from her body. Instantly, she was out of Earth's atmosphere hurling into the never-ending universe.

An intense rushing hum of incredible pitch accelerated past her ears. Into her consciousness formed dizzying images of long-ago memories. Bittersweet times being with her parents, laughing and fighting with her siblings, times of flying with friends and eating with distant cousins, and even jousting with some unfavorable characters in her life. So, also, recollections came of drifting in the remarkable beauty of Earth-life that was deemed her, which she now felt regrets for neglecting due to her own self-exalting desires.

Additionally, an unsettling image of being the only life form in the whole of space barged into her film-of-life even as the stars, planets, and moons blazed passed her. Though careening at unbelievable break-neck speed, she finally came to stand alone on the extensive heights of the cosmos, at once becoming well aware of an incredible emo-tion coursing through her: the daunting and menacing realization that she was truly alone. This despairing mood she thought she was very familiar with, one she thought only she had a monopoly on, came as a shock that, in actuality, she had not truly known loneliness until being surrounded by the extraordinary of everything, and, at the same time, nothing. Life, as she had come to know it, was not around her any-more. She had to believe that her great ancestor Spayro experienced these exact feelings as he went about in search of his own reason for being and living those many, many millennia ago. It's what she was experiencing now.

Yet, in this incredible alien-space realm, Leah was also conscious of the fact that she had gained something of immense value; eagle-eye-sight. Something accorded only a chosen few, certainly not of her own doing. With this new visual perception, she found the capacity to zero-in onto the distant circle of Earth and spied a singular miniscule grain of sand located on top of a massive mountain. This piece was so infinitesimal as to easily be missed if not for light radiating from it. Leah realized that the sun, even from where she was standing a million miles away, did not stop from shining on that great mountain to find a little grain to shine onto.

A flash of lightening instantly burst around Leah and immediately she was thrust back to reality, back to Aquila's mountain, back to the exact place where he was lying, in the same position she had left him. She was shaky and weak inside and out. She looked down at Aquila who gave no clue he had been aware of anything happening to her. He didn't say a word.

*What in the world just happened to me? I know I was gone. I know what I saw.* Leah turned the scenes over and over in her thoughts, scrutinizing them so that she might come to a somewhat believable conclusion. *Am I that speck of sand? And that mountain, is it this one I'm standing on? Was it depicting Aquila as a mountain and me being with him?* A small voice formed softly into her thoughts, words she had heard before. *It's what we see with our good eyes.* Looking again at her feathers, she surmised that her unearthly summit was some sort of sign for her. It could be a warning. But her world was dependent on what she worked hard for. *I need these feathers. They're my feathers, the very things to help me.*

The battle continued inside Leah throughout the rest of the day. Aquila never moved from his position, and he didn't speak to her again. But, there was another matter that held her worried above all others.

*Aquila must be hungry. I know that if he doesn't eat soon he'll get weaker and weaker. But there's no food. He ate all the fish he brought back yesterday. None will appear for him out of thin air, either. And I can't help him in that department. I'm not the kind to go hunting even if I wanted to. This could be the end for him.* She turned and silently cried to herself. She left Aquila alone. Surprisingly, she was thinking about food, needing to keep up her own strength. Her survival instincts were flashing red again, a warning she had to take seriously. Food still remained for her. Her berry branch that Aquila so graciously brought her was near the cave. She slowly trudged toward it. *What am I going to do without him? I won't be able to survive up here alone.*

Leah nibbled listlessly at the fruit, looking up occasionally at the unmoving Golden Eagle. But a decision had to be made, and she made one. If Aquila died, she would leave the mountain and go the way she had decided before. Down there was her way of life, what she knew to stay alive. She shivered. *How can I go back to living the same way after all this? But has anything really changed?* She picked at the berries again that at any other time would have tasted wonderful to a hungry little bird. *Why did this have to happen to him? To me?*

Leah spent the rest the day away from Aquila, not wishing to disturb him. But, at dusk she watched Aquila drag himself, with sheer difficulty and labored breathing, closer to the mouth of the cave. Her silent friend settled down for the night and retreated into himself again. Leah quietly moved inside and lay down for another restless evening. It became colder and her worries deepened as she wondered how Aquila would keep warm. The wind whistled passed the cave's opening, creating an occasional ghostly howl which made her shudder. She ducked farther down into the little nook for any semblance of security she could draw to herself.

# Chapter 16

# RESCUE OF ANOTHER KIND

*The hero is no braver than an ordinary man;*
*But, he is braver five minutes longer.*
*–Ralph Waldo Emerson*

Early the next morning, sitting deep in the cave, Leah desperately wished the chaotic scenes from her dreams would scatter when she stepped outside. Daylight usually does that; lighting all things too dark and too deep that fermented unchecked throughout the still night. But fear didn't leave even as she stood at the cave's opening and shafts of light kissed the white peaks of the mountains.

"Could things really have changed overnight? Could Aquila really be back in shape like he used to be?" Leah's hope for good fortune was barely hanging on as she faced another day. "Of course things haven't changed. Who am I kidding? He couldn't have healed that fast."

Unexpectedly, she heard a whirring sound just outside the cave. It sounded exactly the same like Aquila's massive wings when she saw him landing before. But, Leah knew it couldn't be him. Loose soil on the ledge stirred in a dust cloud. Not even her wildest imagination could help her escape the terror rising in her heart: the scavenging creature had returned to kill Aquila.

"That monster is back!" Leah didn't hesitate; she ran to help Aquila. Anger rose up in her as quickly as her heart beat with panic running through the cave to shield her friend from the attacker. It was the proverbial David-meets-Goliath, but she could think of nothing else. Just as she broke out into the light, looking for the killer, a hefty fish carcass plummeted from the sky, dropping right in front of her. She would have been killed by it, a quick and unflattering death for a sparrow with a dazzling name like *Spizella Passerina*, had she not seen a shadow cover the sun from her.

As Leah accessed the strange occurrence of the fish out of water lying dead high on a mountain, she heard the unmistakable call of an eagle, a sound quite like Aquila's. Searching the sky, she saw a large bird like the one before. She was sure of it. With its wide wings slicing through the current, quickly eating up the space between them, it was a long distance away in no time. She found herself alone once again with Aquila, her pounding heart, and a smelly dead fish. She let out a thin laugh of sheer relief.

"Ha-ha! Imagine that. Food for Aquila did come out of thin air. It wasn't a scavenger bird after all." Leah laughed again. "How wonderful!"

Another amazing thing happened right before her eyes. Aquila rose up slowly and dragged himself toward the fish. This went on every few feet until he finally reached it. Though he struggled tearing at the carcass with his broken beak, Leah could tell he was eating. It was the first time since Aquila's strange behavior that he shifted more than just turning over. He seemed willing enough to eat, though the look of death hung all around him.

*I wonder how that bird knew about Aquila's condition. How did it know where to find him? Well, however it happened, I'm so happy my friend has food to keep him alive and strong. In my book, that stranger is classified a rescuer.*

Aquila was eating, though with great difficulty. And, like magic, Leah could see a tiny change in him. She noticed a slight shaking of his body as though an electrical current pulsated through him. It wasn't a frightening thing, but something of great hope. Life seemed to slowly seep back into her ailing friend, including Leah's heart that had almost lost all confidence of seeing the Golden Eagle revive.

A spark of light shone in Aquila's eyes as he looked at Leah. She moved closer to him. She saw it in his eyes. She could feel it all around her. There was no mistaking it; the gleam of strength shone in his golden-brown globes again. Leah stood quietly for a few seconds, arguing to herself whether to speak to him or just leave him alone. But, she couldn't stand the silent treatment any longer.

"Aquila? Aquila, can you talk?"

"Leah," Aquila whispered, his tone still edged in tiredness.

*He said my name!* "What happened to you? Who did this to you?"

Aquila closed his eyes and let out a long, slow breath, as though contemplating whether to let out his secret to her. He opened his eyes once again and gently held her in them.

"*I* did this...to me," Aquila said, matter-of-factly.

Her mouth dropped open. "I don't understand, Aquila. Why would you...how could you...?" She was at a loss for words. "Why?"

Aquila again settled down onto the warm ground. He had finished all he wanted to eat, although to Leah it didn't seem enough. The sun once again peaked over the mountains, and as though it was looking for Aquila, it settled down peacefully on him. He seemed ready to answer her questions; a mystery he didn't need to keep any longer from his nervous little ward. He spoke in a slow and labored manner.

"Leah, I am an eagle and there are certain times...eagles have to renew themselves. With all the flying...all the hunting, all the beating up from the elements...on our bodies, we need time...time to rejuvenate. The noise in the cave...I'm sure you heard it. It was me. I was breaking...my beak, brittle from so much use. I was scraping off...my weak talons. You saw the feathers on the floor. I had to pull out the old, worn ones...tattered ones. If I hadn't, it would have greatly hindered my flying and...ultimately...my life." Aquila stopped to rest.

Leah stood speechless, astounded at what Aquila was sharing with her.

"Don't...be shocked, Leah. It's as normal to me as it is to you and your kind when molting...only on a larger scale. You see, you and I... we live differently, in different environments...with different ways of flying, different food to catch and to eat. And along with battling the elements, it all...takes its toll." Aquila paused to take several short breaths of air. His head was slightly off the ground, twisted upward to look directly at Leah. "An eagle must renew himself, Leah, if...if he is going to survive. So every few years we go to a secluded place... and we begin the process...I just explained." He laid his head back onto the ground.

It had to be true. Aquila wouldn't lie to her. But she still could not get accustomed to the fact that the once beautiful creature she only met yesterday could have had such a quick metamorphosis. She remembered her earlier observations as it festered in her thoughts again.

*But this...this molting business sure makes him look kind of...*

"Ugly?" Aquila said.

Leah jumped backwards as a tiny chirp escaped her mouth. Although embarrassed, she thought she heard a faint chuckle from Aquila.

"I'm sorry, Aquila. I wasn't trying to be mean about it, but..." Leah stopped. "How do you do that?"

"Do what?"

"That! What you just did. You read my thoughts. Again! I was only thinking it. I know I didn't say it out loud."

"Oh, that," Aquila said, with a slight lilt in his voice. "Well...I'm different that way." He took a deep breath, and in a more serious note said, "Let's just say it's a...a...special ability."

"It's so weird."

"It's a gift," Aquila emphasized again, "and I do not take it lightly. I don't expect you to understand it." Then he added, "But, if I hadn't had this gift I never would have..."

"Never would have what, Aquila?"

"I never would have found you."

The unfolding of her life, once more revealed by this curious sage, amazed her. "You mean you could see me whenever I was in trouble?"

"More *feel* than see you, Leah. I could feel your pain as I flew... the expanse of this territory. I sensed your distress...especially during those close calls of death."

Leah looked at Aquila with a new sense of awe and admiration. Even what she had judged as ugly about him—his torn and weak body—was now more beautiful than ever, because now she saw him with her inner eyes; her good eyes. She could see past all the physical shock and see the true Aquila.

"So you were, in reality, my watchman."

"I *am* a watchman!" Aquila said with a strong voice. "I am the keeper of the expanse."

It was the first time Leah detected any energy in him past all the emotional and disturbing changes stemming from his harsh, though necessary, transformation, as she had come to understand it.

Aquila continued. "The world of nature was made for its beauty and its fruits, Leah. We, the bird kingdom, were also made to add to that beauty…covering the sky with song and grace. But when there is disharmony in the air…when one is in distress, there is a break in the atmosphere, a discord in the way of life. It's much like if it would snow in summer, it would be noticed…because it is out of sync. It is in discord and disharmony…far from the way of true nature."

Leah noticed that he was taking fewer breaths as he talked. She was more convinced that she would see Aquila back to normal, if she could call it that, because nothing was normal to her on this mountaintop.

"The other bird you saw and heard was an eagle, too. He knew what was going on when he spotted me. He understood. That's why he brought me…food. He's gone through it, through the same thing. He knew what to do when he spotted me." Pausing, Aquila looked up to the sky as though searching for the lifesaver that dropped manna from heaven for him. "We take care of each other that way."

The sun traveled through the sky quickly that day. She was happier, and the reason she was happier was because Aquila's future looked brighter. After their long conversation, she let him rest under the powerful healing agents of the sun. He moved with a little more agility from strength the food provided him. Leah was better able to enjoy her own berries, too. The stress that enveloped her from worry and fear slowly dissipated like steam off the heated ground after a short rainfall.

Aquila dragged himself into the cave. The moon was showing its fuller girth in the late month. He went inside only as far as the sunlight had beamed its hot waves onto the ground. It would keep his body warm throughout the cooling night. But, Leah began imagining a different kind of evil presenting itself against the still weak eagle.

*He's still pretty vulnerable out here. What if a wild beast comes during the night and attacks him?* A shiver ran down her back. *I have to keep watch over him. I need to. It's the least I can do.* Leah's thoughts for a rescue quickened toward a plan. *I'm going to stay outside tonight in Aquila's giant nest. It's the best thing to do. It has a good vantage point for spying any stalking predators.* She could hear Aquila's feathers rustling as he settled for the night. *I can easily detect any slight movement outside the cave, as they would have to pass the distance between me and Aquila. I still don't know what I can do if a beast really tries to attack him, but I am determined to do anything it takes. He would do no less for me.*

Leah paused, tears welling up at the edge of her eyes, as she remembered what Aquila did for her. She was alive and he was the reason for it. She climbed the tall nest, steadying herself with outstretched wings, holding a moan of pain at her still tender shoulder. The moon shined luminously as though for Leah's sake. She was the watchman tonight, and she could see clearly. Occasional white wispy clouds curled in slow motion across the skyline like smoke, filtering the silvery light. She looked out from her post toward the more northern mountains. By the moon's glow, she could see the faraway peaks outlined in an opalescent sheen.

Once again the unusual sounds drifted toward Leah, whispers of ancient music rebounding off the barriers and walls of the mountains. They blew into her spirit the joy of being alive, igniting in her a knowing that she was a big part of it all. She was beginning to believe she was even a bigger part than the mountains themselves. Leah didn't know why this thought came to her. She couldn't imagine being significant at all compared to these wondrous land giants. But, she knew deep inside that, yes, she was very important to the whole of nature. Aquila had told her so, and it made her feel very important.

Leah filtered through the last few days of her life as the moon climbed higher through the night. It was something she would never have believed in a million years had it not happened to her. She was standing on the rim of a giant nest trying to watch over and protect a bird that was at least ten times larger than she was.

*How out of sync is this picture?* A slight giggle rushed out. She quickly slapped her wings over her mouth, scolding herself for making noise. It could have awakened Aquila or, worse yet, alerted an enemy lurking close by. She settled herself into a small indentation of the nest's rim. She and Aquila had a better day today. Leah wondered how long it would take Aquila to heal and how long she would be on the mountain.

There was something going on outside the nest, something like steps quietly brushing along on the hard, sun-dried ground. Slowly and quietly, Leah sat up. In the moon's glowing aura she could see a sinister creature sneaking toward Aquila's leftover meal which had remained outside the cave. Leah was horrified. The smell from the rotting meat had alerted the animal for it to investigate in their direction. She began shaking. She was hoping the animal was there only to grab the meal and leave, hoping she would have to do nothing but wait.

Shame quickly filled her. She had purposely stayed outside to defend Aquila, but now she could only think about the choking fear at her throat. It was easier and safer for her to wish the thief only wanted the food and then it'd go away without any trouble, without any kind of altercation. But, a more horrible scenario crossed her mind.

*What if that thing attacks Aquila, instead! Animals can detect weaker ones, and Aquila's hardly able to defend himself at all.* The night's glow revealed a creature with thick, black fur that glistened as she watched it crawl to the remains of the food. *What will Aquila do if the other eagle doesn't return for a few days...or doesn't return at all? He might not know that Aquila still needs food.* The thought of the rescue eagle's probable oversight made her heart sick. She couldn't bear seeing her friend suffer anymore. *I've just got to do something and the less stress and commotion for Aquila the better. He's probably deeper into the cave now so hopefully he won't hear anything.*

Aquila had already taught her that she must not only sail above the turbulent winds of life, but at times, in sailing through them, she would become even stronger. After all, the winds do eventually die out. Even in Aquila's state of mind, when she first saw him so disfigured, she noticed he chose to face the sun, to face the situation, and not hide in his dark secluded cave all by himself. That way others saw his situation and reached out to help. He swallowed any pride he might have held and accepted that help.

*I chose to hide away from those who tried to help me. I was a loner. I didn't want anyone around me except those whose feathers I could gain. That was pretty selfish of me.* She watched as the creature grabbed the meat in its mouth and began to drag it away. *Well, one consolation about all that I've gone through is that I've gained some courage. I've got to stop that food thief.* She had contrived an idea from watching Aquila. *I'll use the element of surprise. I can pummel that intruder with whatever I can hold. Along with that, I can belt out a high-pitched shriek catching it off guard and scare it away. It'd wish it had never even thought to intrude on our domain.* Leah was surprised at her notion of the mountaintop being her domain, but Aquila accepted her so readily that it gave her the feeling of belonging. *Well, I guess I've grown accustomed to this place. Aquila saw to it that I would know he accepted me. He showed nothing but kindness from the very beginning.*

It was time for action. Leah dropped to the floor of the nest and gathered some small stones in one of her claws and a small cluster of twigs in the other from the nest's accumulated debris. Both were plentiful in the huge old nest from years of use. The small arsenal would not hurt the beast, but it would catch it off guard.

Leah struggled up to the rim of the nest and stood for a few seconds. It reminded her of the first time she was on the rim of her own nest as a birdling learning how to fly. She inhaled a deep breath and plunged toward the prowler. Forgetting her damaged wing in the desire to rescue her friend, she immediately felt a sharp pain shoot through her. But there was no turning back. Flying above the creature, she opened her claws to release the implements of war. At the same time she let out a high-pitched screech and, to her own surprise, she flew down at the animal, pecking at its unprotected head. The beast let out a terrified grunt and dropped the food. It backed away quickly, stumbling over big rocks, falling onto a descending pathway along the wall's edge. It tumbled end over end for a few feet, narrowly escaping falling over the ledge into the darkness of the forest floor below.

Leah flew back onto the edge of Aquila's nest with pounding heart, straining her eyes to see what the animal would do. Would it retaliate? But, after regaining its balance, the panicked creature quickly scampered away without a backward glance.

"It worked!" Leah exclaimed. She cringed as she wondered whether all the commotion had awakened Aquila, but she heard nothing from inside the cave. She felt a little disappointed. He would never know the surprising bravado that rose up within her to defend him. But, then, no one really had to know but she herself, for it had benefited her as much as it did Aquila. She was made out of tougher material than she thought. The meal remained, but more importantly, Aquila was safe.

*Now, he can still have his breakfast in the morning.* Though thoroughly satisfied with her great achievement, she didn't envy Aquila having putrid fish for breakfast, but she was grateful that it was available.

Vital signs of recovery were more evident in Aquila as the days passed, and Leah detected, with great joy, those changes. He regained daily strength in the use of his beak and talons, making it easier to grasp the food dropped down periodically to him from the sky angel. Once more his massive feathers shined with health, groomed to perfection to capture its full beauty. He would stand for long periods of time along the ledge (dangerously close as far as Leah was concerned for someone still not strong enough to sail the infinite blue space) and look pensively out at the clear skies or down to the world below them.

She was looking forward to the time that he would finally look as magnificent as when she first met him. *He's almost Aquila again,* Leah thought happily as she stood beside him on the ledge.

"I was *always* Aquila," the Golden Eagle asserted. He turned to face Leah.

Leah's heart skipped a beat as she heard his strong voice reply to her thoughts. She was still not used to the uncanny gift he had.

"What I am inside never changed because of what happened to me on the outside, my dear little sparrow. My inside is my true self. Though my outside changed, it didn't alter what I am on the inside. I am who I am. Always." Leah listened deliberately. His voice was now clear and strong as ever. "Leah, there are some who desperately want to change what is on the outside because they don't like who they really are on the inside. But, when it can't be done, there is a power struggle within. The more powerful controller will always take over, because it is usually based on judgmental attitudes about self. It's really an uncontrolled control, if you know what I mean, Leah, a raging war inside one's mind screaming for who they really are."

"But, Aquila, how does one truly know who they are?" Leah asked with a desperate plea in her voice. She had been searching for the answer for a long time.

"Ah, sweet Leah, that question is as ageless as the mountains."

She could almost believe that Aquila had the answers she was seeking. He looked out into the sky again with a longing that told Leah he missed being a part of the endless sky for these many long days he's been in recovery. With the snowy-white clouds lazily floating by, it was as though he was waiting for the wind to call out his name. Slowly, his body began swaying back and forth, moving to the wind's rhythm.

*It's as though he was flying right now,* Leah thought.

"Yes, a bird is lost without his ability to fly," Aquila said. "But renewal is a necessary part of life, Leah. It's a must; it gets rid of the old useless things to make way for the new. You see, a caterpillar desires to become a beautiful butterfly someday, but it must go through some transformations before it can become so." Aquila looked squarely at his little charge. "To continue about your life question…" He spread out his wings a little to again capture the hot rays of the sun, still regenerating his body with the heat. "When we compare ourselves to others it indicates that we don't really know who we are, and therefore don't like who we are. So, then, begins the search for something that is unattainable, and life becomes an agonizing journey."

Leah looked down onto the ground, fidgeting uncomfortably, knowing Aquila's description was too close to her heart for comfort.

"But, when we look at ourselves with good eyes, truly believe we were made for something special, it means we come to believe in ourselves and who we really are. So, then, we're happy to go out into the world every day just as we are. It's like looking at your reflection in a pool of water, Leah. When a pebble is dropped into it and causes ripples, your reflection on the surface is carried on forever, carried out into the fullness of that ripple. It becomes a larger, fuller wave of you for the whole world to see, to see the true you, because your reflection does not lie." Then, he added softly, "Leah."

Leah was entranced by Aquila's keen insights. He was painting her a picture of truth. She remembered looking into the little puddle of water when she was in that huge forest shocked at what she had seen. Staring back at her was someone she didn't know, someone she didn't even recognize. Thoughts screamed through her mind as she recalled the agonizing picture. *How could I have been blind to what was happening to me? I'd become a miserable little puppet in my own hands and I didn't even know it. These feathers hadn't turned out the way I had hoped they would. It's all been more torment than treasure. Nothing prepared me for the horrible things that happened to me.*

"Leah," Aquila whispered again.

Leah jerked her head up; surprised she had forgotten Aquila was standing in front of her. Totally lost in her thoughts, in her loss, even a whisper was a shock to her senses. She saw great and tender concern fixed on Aquila's face.

"Leah, don't beat yourself up for what's happened. The past is gone. Let it go. Thinking about it will only keep your mind bound and your spirit grounded."

With shock, Leah watched Aquila spread out his massive wings and began flapping them at a slow pace. He continued faster and faster until it was all Leah could do from being blown over. Then, he opened his mouth. Leah prepared herself for what was coming next. Placing her wings over her head, she covered her ears. Aquila's deafening cry pierced through every fiber of her being, sinking deeply into her spirit with the realization that she, too, could overcome her trials just as Aquila overcame his. With the gusting wind all about her, Leah knew his strength had returned. She felt invigorated, shivering as though a cold blast of winter snow pummeled her. High energy surged through her, traveling from her head down through her feathers and finally to the tip of her tail. It felt as though the weight of pain and loss and all her fears were swept away.

Aquila stopped, and Leah straightened up. She had been leaning into his forceful gale. Heaving a big sigh of relief, she opened her eyes and straightened up to face the eagle.

"Leah, look down on the ground."

With a puzzled look on her face, she did as he said. A shriek flew out of her mouth. "Aquila! My new feathers!"

Lying at her feet were the feathers Leah had painstakingly searched for and glued onto her body. They looked so disagreeable to her now; dull and lifeless. Gone was the glitter and sparkle that captured her the first time she laid eyes on them. Leah remembered Aquila sharing with her about the feathers he discarded periodically for the sake of his own life. It's always with great pain, but an integral part to living life wholly.

"Now watch this!" Aquila cried out. He again began his steady stream of plowing wings, and Leah watched as the gust picked up the loose feathers in its maelstrom. The feathers began a twirling dance, like a ballet, toward the brink of the ledge. After a few second's hold, they fell over the cliff and were instantly caught up in the mountain's vortex, scattering them in different directions. Leah ran to the edge as soon as Aquila stopped his onslaught, watching the feathers furl away through the air.

Standing breathless, watching with awe as the feathers disappeared, Leah felt something else lift from her. Gone was the significance that she had desired with each one, the desire to become someone she wasn't. Gone was the dark shroud that encased her in doubt about herself for so long. All these invisible yet weighty things drifted out and away from her, close behind the feathers, and into the vast eternal sky. Freedom came to her like that first gleam at dawn, shining brighter and brighter until the fullness of day is welcomed.

"I can't believe it!" Leah yelled happily, spreading her wings out, twirling around over and over as though to embrace the whole world. "I feel free! I feel free to be a sparrow, the Chipping Sparrow that I was meant to be. The beautiful..." Leah stopped, embarrassed with herself.

"Go on, Leah! Say it!" Aquila encouraged. Leah turned around to face Aquila. "Say it, and believe it. You're free. Say it. Free to be the beautiful little Chipping Sparrow you were meant to be."

Leah was no longer surprised of Aquila's ability to know her thoughts. She was exhilarated that he thought her to be beautiful. With a firm shake of her head in agreement, she turned to face the world from the mountaintop.

"I...am...beautiful!" It carried out over the pale blue expanse for the entire kingdom to hear. She was announcing truth about herself with her good eyes. And for the first time ever she believed it. "I...am...a...beautiful...Chipping...Sparrow!"

"Good for you, Leah!" Aquila chimed in. "Now you sound sure of yourself. I am very proud of you, my little one." Aquila moved up to the ledge next to her. "You see, we know only in part what life consists of, and what we think about ourselves can either make us or break us in this life. There is power in words, Leah, especially those we think about ourselves. When we speak the truth with our good eyes, then nothing will stop us from accomplishing all we can be and do."

Leah had been staring up into Aquila's grand shape silhouetted against the light of the sun the entire time he was speaking. She was engrossed in his words, his healing words. That's what they were to her—words that healed her wounded spirit, heart, and mind. Aquila lived what he said. His words were truth and life to her. She had never felt safer than she did now.

"Do you understand, Leah?"

"Yes, I do, Aquila. I just wish I had known sooner and spared myself so much pain."

"Well, just look at it this way. You can start to change the past by the way you think and speak about yourself from now on, just like you did a minute ago. That's a great start."

"Yes, it is," Leah whispered. She found that she could believe anything from this remarkable Golden Eagle. He had proved it over and over to her.

The day wore on slowly and delicately as the friends sat contemplating all that had transpired in the many days since the two met on the mountaintop. In a quiet moment, Leah sat pondering a thought that came to her.

*How in the world, out of the whole kingdom of birds, was I the one to meet as magnificent a bird as Aquila, and still remain alive? In fact, I'm even more alive now than I ever was. I had been dictating life from the outside in, rather than from the inside out. I can see the difference now.*

Aquila began to feed on the quarry left by the rescuing eagle as Leah looked at the receding sun. The stranger had continued flying overhead periodically throughout Aquila's healing, depositing food for him. But, as she watched the kind eagle sail away yesterday, she felt it was the last time she would ever see him again. She came to sincerely appreciate the sacred law of the eagles. She could not even bring herself to think what Aquila would have suffered if the eagle-rescuer had not found him.

The day had been an eventful one. Leah viewed the sun's final descent. Within a few minutes it was a fiery orange glow in the horizon and, immediately, twilight was on the mountain. She made her way into the huge nest. She wanted to sleep outside under the sparkling blanket of the night. She somehow felt this was the last night she would be spending in this eagle's kingdom. The sounds changed in the clear night; the song of the mountains played by the ever-moving winds softly swept by Leah. From somewhere far away off the shores of the Big Waters intermittent sounds of bells clanged. She looked toward the west where the receding light was resting somewhere faraway where her home was.

*It's been so long since I've been home. How can I ever get used to living down there after experiencing all this up here?*

# Chapter 17
## THE TRIP HOME

*Greater love hath no man than this,*
*That a man lay down his life for his friends.*
*- Gospel of John*

Time quickly passed, yet Leah sensed that a total season of life had been given to her on a silver platter. Beginning from the time she came in the spring to where she was now, sitting on top of a mountain in an enormous nest of a giant Golden Eagle, her friend had always been a part of the equation. She just didn't know it until now.

Although overjoyed that Aquila's trying ordeal had come to an end, she knew another end had come. It was no surprise to her that this spectacular respite in her life was taking yet another turn. She had come to dread this turn in the road, but it was time to go home and face life as it came her way. The same way Aquila faced all of life—with good eyes, love, and acceptance. But, would she be able to do it without him? It seemed so much easier when she was in his presence.

Aquila came out from the cave. Leah watched quietly as he climbed up onto the edge of the nest and turned to face her without saying a word; a looming stature of power and mystery. Clouds were coming in from the northwest. They were full, non-threatening clouds shrouding the mountains in a dusky gray hue. It was another signal to Leah that summer was nearer to its end. Soon the cooler autumn winds would be blowing. She looked at the dreary clouds above her, now seeing them with good eyes, concluding that nothing changes behind them. The sun still shines in its brilliance, though a little obstructed. Looking at Aquila standing across from her, something else big and great was going to shine through. Leah was sure of it.

Still without a word, Aquila opened his magnificent wings and began a slow back and forth waving in front of her. Intrigued, she watched as he continued the forceful action, blowing air in her face, pinning her against protruding limbs of the nest. He began uttering short, high-pitched screeches into the air. Aquila lifted up and hovered over the nest just as Leah had seen her own mother bird do when the time had come to teach the siblings how to fly. Leah remembered a great desire to do the same thing her mother was doing. Although fear had played a big part that had almost cost her to achieve a very important element of her life, this was unquestionably different. She watched Aquila come back down onto the edge of the nest.

"Come on, Leah!" he cried out. There was a sparkle of fun in his eyes as he looked at her. "It's time."

"Time?" Leah couldn't believe it. She looked at his plowing wings. "Time for what? You mean to fly? Together? Are you sure you're strong enough?"

"Strong enough?" Aquila bellowed with laughter. "Of course, I'm strong enough. I've never been better."

Leah let out a small, nervous chuckle. Then another worry crossed her mind. "But if I fly next to you, I'll be blown away!"

"Don't worry, sweet Leah, I'll hold you up with my wings. I've never lost any of my little ones."

*He's never lost any of his little ones? I wonder if he means eagle children of his own. Or could he have helped others like me from the bird kingdom that got into trouble out there in the world? I wonder if they also flew with him. Did he carry them on his wings?* Leah looked hard at her big friend. He was ready to fly just as soon as she said the word. *If he's all I've come to know him to be, then, yes, he's helped others like me. That's who he is.*

"Ok, Aquila, my big friend." Leah yelled above the whooshing sound. "I'm ready to follow you."

"Great! Now come up here to the rim."

Her wing was finally repaired from its injury. She could now concentrate on flying with him without the worry and without the pain. She did as she was told.

With a booming screech, Aquila yelled, "Let's go!"

He flew off the nest, suddenly descending, but caught an updraft, floating smoothly out and away from the mountain wall. Leah immediately thought how he reminded her of the delightful kite the humans flew on the beach at the Big Waters. It was such carefree and smooth sailing.

*But a string doesn't hold Aquila. He's the freest thing I've ever known. And, by the looks of it, I can see there's nothing to worry about. He is strong enough.*

Leah hesitated as she heard the wind against the mountain. Watching Aquila hold himself in place, his tail and wings expertly turning, Leah held her breath. He looked intently at her, patiently waiting, as she returned his gaze.

With a loud voice, she shouted, "Here I come!" Leah flew off the ledge and into the swirling current of invisible waves. Immediately, she felt liberated using her wings again. "Oh, how wonderful it feels!" Most importantly, she hadn't given thought to the new feathers, long gone into obscurity. Leah flew toward Aquila who was flying farther from the mountain face for her sake. She made her way up next to him, staying by his side as she adjusted to the full freedom of flight once again. Though it seemed like eternity being grounded for so long, the freedom felt grand as she maneuvered herself along with the brisk wind.

But, then, a shifting current caught her up and away from Aquila. Her heart went to her throat. Swallowing hard, she heroically maneuvered back and forth until she was beside him, again. Aquila never lost sight of her, allowing just enough time for her against the buffeting airstream to make her own way back before he felt she needed his help.

"That's the way, Leah," Aquila said, laughing as he cheered her on. "You're back in fine shape."

Leah laughed. "So are you!"

With a more serious tone, he said, "Follow me, Leah. It's time to take you home."

A jolt shot in her chest almost as hard as the impact from the fleeing rabbit; only this hit was straight to her heart. She wasn't prepared to hear that. Everything good for her had taken place up there on the mountain. How she wished that certain spans of time spent with others weren't toward an end of things. But time doesn't stop for anyone, and now it was time to go back down.

"Ok, Aquila. I'm ready," she said softly, though she was not telling the whole truth.

"Good girl, my little sparrow." Aquila gently guided the huge pinions of his left wing under her tiny body. Barely touching her, she still felt a part of his big life, part of his big mountain, and part of the vast sky that he commanded as she flew beside him. Leah then heard a familiar voice deep inside her.

*I will always carry you, Leah, if you let me. Never forget that, my sweet friend.*

Leah knew she didn't hear it audibly, but she knew it was Aquila; a whisper as light and breezy as the unseen wind, yet with the ability to feel it. She accepted it as his words of love to her, a voice she would always cherish. They glided on the smooth stream that easily carried them west toward her terrain. Leah looked down toward earth and was awestruck at the astounding landscape below her. She could clearly see that she had not been welcoming nature's beauty outside her own world, and now it was as though she was seeing it for the first time.

The two companions were slowly descending as they approached the area where Leah encountered both the Bobcat and, ultimately, her lifesaver in person. With Aquila, Leah knew it would be a non-stop flight to where she lived. He could do it. But the flight from the mountain was already taking its toll on her as she was still too weakened from little prior flying. Aquila sensed her struggle.

"Leah, climb on my back. I'll carry you."

Leah's eyes expanded in shock. "But...but how can I do that, Aquila? What if I miss? I won't be able to gain control quickly enough. I'll fall to the ground like a stone and...and..."

"Leah," Aquila said firmly. He wanted to divert her attention engrossed in fear back onto him. "Listen to me."

"I'm sorry, Aquila. I lost my head for a second there."

"Believe me when I say you can do it. You've proven to yourself that you're stronger than you think. I'll slow down into hover mode so you can easily fly above me. Then, as soon as you settle on my back, grab hold of my feathers and crouch down. That way the wind won't hit you square on. Trust me, it will be amazing."

Leah still hesitated. She had already come so far in trusting Aquila but, as she looked at the tree land far below, she shivered.

"Leah, look at me," Aquila said with a strong voice again, his head turned, looking intently at her.

Leah forced her eyes away from the great distance below and focused on Aquila.

"Do you trust me?" He held an edge of concern in his voice.

Leah realized that this was where she always went wrong. She knew Aquila well enough now to be trusted; he had done so much to help her. So why did she always come to question him? That same gentle inner voice came to her heart.

*You think you can only trust yourself, but you've got to realize that it takes letting go of the familiar thing for you to fully understand the better thing. It takes letting go of everything else that you ever thought essential to exist and trust in something bigger than you.*

"Letting go is trusting in me, Leah." Aquila said. "So I ask you again—do you trust me?"

Without hesitation, Leah let go. She had to. She saw it in his good eyes that she could do it. She sailed over Aquila's back and lowered herself until she landed between his shoulders. Aquila reduced his speed enough to allow her ample time to execute the daunting feat. In the wide open sky, higher than she's ever been, Leah was carried by something bigger than her.

"I did it!"

Aquila chuckled. "Yes, you did."

Leah grabbed tightly onto his feathers and lay low as he had told her. Without warning and with accelerating speed, Aquila began a wide, counter clock-wise flight. But, they weren't spiraling downward toward home as she had expected. They were traveling upwards, farther and farther into the endless blue. Leah couldn't believe it, but she wasn't going to ask him why they were going higher than the mountains where he lived. Aquila's confident power and strong demeanor gave her confidence that they would be safe no matter how high.

She held on tightly as they continued climbing, driving his wings rhythmically to keep above the summer tide that carried them. *I'm not accustomed to flying so high.* Leah chuckled. *How ironic that I, a bird, find it very strange to fly this high.* She found it both startling and exciting at the same time.

Aquila continued climbing and encountered thick cloud cover that seemed it would block further flight. But he zoomed through the misty white. Quietness hung all around them as though they were the only two creatures on the face of the earth. As Aquila leveled off, she saw a most spectacular sight—the topside of the clouds. Captivated by the row upon row of gray and white softness, the clouds extended westward toward the hazy sun, radiating an ocean of effervescent glow.

"Oooh," Leah whispered. "It's so beautiful up here, Aquila. I've never seen anything so incredible." Then, looking down at her rescuer, she added, "Well, except for you, of course." Aquila smiled. "It's like touching heaven."

"Yes, Leah, it certainly seems that way, doesn't it?"

She looked in every direction. It was limitless. The sun shined a hushed golden atmosphere all around them. They were silent for a long time, only the swish of Aquila's wings cutting softly through the still air was heard. Then, Leah spoke in a hushed tone. She didn't want to disturb the sacredness of the moment. "Aquila, do you come up here often?"

"Yes, I do. Quite often, in fact. I need to. It helps remind me to keep looking at the earthly things from a higher perspective to help me live my life down there."

*He needs to do that? He's so perfect. Why does he need help living out a phenomenal life like his?*

"It's how one sees life to live it, Leah," Aquila said. "Remember the good eyes I told you about? My species and a few other large birds of the world are the only ones that can climb to these great heights, and we are masters at taking advantage of it." Aquila expertly dropped down through the clouds once again. "Look down there, Leah. What do you see?"

"I can see the whole world!"

The land was in quilt-patch pattern as the summer months showed its colors in the farmland fields. Various shades of green and yellow dotted the landscape as the farm-fresh plants began their move toward harvesting. The land was marked off in blocks as gray roads criss-crossed throughout the territory separating fields, farms, towns, and wilderness. An occasional white steeple of a church stabbed through the tall monuments of trees and small town buildings. The land swelled up and down with smooth green hills and rocky low lands giving the earth a wrinkled look. Murky rivers flowed alongside hills and through valleys, under bridges and through towns as though trying to find a place to rest.

Aquila and Leah had long cleared the huge forest that lay at the foot of the mountains. She turned her head to look behind her. The large body of blue-gray water lay cloaking the earth in a stunning, dreamy look of beginning and end, where the sky and water met, where the colors barely distinguished themselves one from the other. She was enthralled by the water as she was with the land below her.

Aquila asked her again. "What do you see, Leah?"

"Everything," she exclaimed. But then she added more solemnly, "And not everything. There's something missing." Leah could feel Aquila's body quiver underneath her as he chuckled. "It seems I can see the whole world, Aquila, but I can't see the living, breathing, moving things; the animals and humankind from way up here."

"Good observation, little sparrow. Yes, from here we can see the whole world at a glance, sort of speak, and everything looks beautiful and peaceful, even harmless. But up here we can tend to forget the rest of the living kingdom."

"You mean we have to remember that there will always be others we come in contact with, don't you?"

"Yes. But, if we keep this high perspective when we are down there on earth, at closer contact with other living things, we won't overlook their own beauty around us. It's the beauty of the positive things that we focus on that keeps us thinking good, Leah, not the ugliness of the negative things. Of course, there is danger down there, like that wildcat in the forest. But, even he is a regal creature created for a purpose and we need only to be careful around him, to give him his space. So, if we live life agreeably, we can then live it with purpose, also. It all has to do with the good eyes, Leah. Remember that."

"Yes, Aquila, with good eyes. I'll try my best. Thank you for bringing me up here."

"It has been my greatest pleasure to serve you, Leah Sparrow."

As they flew through the high open sky, Leah remembered that Aquila had kept his promise to her. He had told her at their very first meeting, "I won't eat you, I'll feed you." He had indeed fed her; fed her with the good things of life in her heart, mind, and spirit. On his wings, they were a part of the sky, a cloud, so effortless and light.

"Remember, Leah, one always needs rest from everyday life. As I've shown you that place up there above the clouds, no one can go up there on a whim. But, the grace of that special place will be in your heart forever, to help you through the rough times of life. I came here before I went through my physical and emotional spell back there, but I kept that sacredness in my heart throughout that whole ordeal. I needed that."

"In my heart." Leah contemplated it as she focused on the peace she was feeling. "I guess that if I had grown accustomed to thinking such dark things about myself for so long, I can certainly begin to believe better things for me now."

"Yes, you can, Leah. I have every confidence you will."

Aquila was silent again for a long period. Leah had the uncanny feeling that he was up to something again. Still holding on tightly and laying low, she didn't know what to expect from him, but it became apparent to her that she wouldn't have it any other way concerning her friend. Thousands of feet high, Aquila and his passenger glided along, like a sailing vessel on quiet waters. As the evening sun shifted below the clouds, its lowering radiance painted the land with an enhanced clearer hue. Leah let out a sigh.

*All of this has been so wonderful with Aquila. I'll never forget those days on the mountain-top with him, how he came out of that hard time and how our sky-angel helped him. Now here's this mind-boggling flight over the clouds and I can see the whole world from way up here. What else is there for me to see, to let me know how much he cares for me?*

"Leah, do you want to see something else?" Aquila asked. His mysterious gift of knowing her thoughts still amazed Leah, shaking her quickly out of her meditation.

"Oh! I wasn't really asking out loud."

"You might even ask what else could we possibly do now?"

"Aquila, I haven't asked you anything at all."

"Well, do you want to know?"

She wasn't so sure if her little heart could withstand any more surprises. A familiar feeling crept over her as she remembered the time her mother told her it was time to learn how to fly. It had been a terrifying sensation. She's become acquainted enough with Aquila to know that there was more to their flight home than he had let on. But, she didn't have any more time to muse on the growing alarm inside her, because she could feel Aquila doing something different. It was as though he could no longer control the desire of total abandonment into renewed freedom, of commanding the skies again.

"Leah, answer me!" the eagle cried enthusiastically.

Leah had not witnessed such excitement in Aquila as she did now. She felt if she didn't answer him, he would explode. It made her chuckle. She didn't want to disappoint him.

"OK, Aquila, show me!"

With great exuberance, he cried out, "That's my girl. But you'll have to hold on tighter than ever."

"What?"

"We're going on a wild ride!"

"A wild ride!" she screamed. "I thought we were already on a wild ride!"

Aquila laughed as he banked to his left, away from the ceiling of the sky. Once more, he made a wide circular motion, keeping his slanted position.

"Hold...on!"

Instantly, he began a flat out and rapid free-falling descent through the air; twisting, tumbling, and twirling as though he had gone mad. Leah shut her eyes tight. The wind whistled passed her ears, an incessant whir of a thousand bees. Aquila continued falling contorting his body as though trying to pry Leah off of him, though she had to trust that was not his intention. She suppressed a scream. She wanted more than ever to believe she could face anything. Aquila was the pilot on this flight, after all.

Aquila periodically opened his huge wings for a speedy shift into another position, taking only milliseconds, and continued the frightening down fall. Leah caught short glimpses of earth getting closer at each interval, when she had the nerve to open her eyes at all. Many times she couldn't see anything as Aquila hung upside down, the force of the air plastering her ever tighter against his back. She knew it was altogether impossible to let go and fly away even if she wanted to. She would easily be slammed against his hulking body and be crushed.

Then an astounding feeling of oneness drifted into her spirit even as they hurled toward the ground. Without question, she couldn't help but be a part of this physical insanity instigated by a crazed eagle. She believed Aquila wanted her to experience something hallowed with him; to see and feel the extraordinary world through someone else's eyes and so to capture that spirit of freedom for herself. She felt she had learned to understand his ways. They were higher ways and higher thoughts than hers had ever been. Leah braved one more look toward the ground that quickly closed at every maddening turn Aquila made.

*Only great trust in him will see me through to the end, whatever end that will be.* Leah again squeezed her eyes shut as she caught a swift glimpse of the fast approaching land. Then, without warning, a jolting lurch shook her forcing her to emit a short high squeal. Aquila opened his wings and caught an envelope of wind which instantly turned their riotous spinning into a smooth, level glide again. The chaos was over. She blew out a long sigh of relief, thrilled that both she and the Golden Eagle had been spared a close encounter with solid ground.

"What did you think about that, Leah?" Aquila said, breathlessly.

"That was incredible! But what was so amazing is that I wasn't really afraid-afraid. Do you know what I mean?" she exclaimed. "I mean I knew I could have gone sailing off uncontrollably into space and eventually crash to the ground if I didn't hold on tightly. Of that I was afraid. But, it was an incredible feeling...flying so totally free. I have never experienced that before. But the weirdest part of all, Aquila, was that it felt like you and I were one, like nothing in the world could separate us. Like nothing else in the whole world mattered," she said, stopping enough to catch her breath. "It was amazing!"

"I told you it would be amazing, my little sparrow," Aquila said, laughing. He beamed with pride. "You see, as one begins to trust, especially through the hardest times of life, that trust carries them through and helps turn things around to where life can be more a thrilling challenge than a fearsome obstacle. But," Aquila added emphatically, "the choice is still ours of how we see life to live it."

"Yes...good eyes."

Leah knew this truth well now as it settled into her heart like the many other words she had devoured from her friend's wealth of wisdom. She began seeing his words as jewels. Jewels for her crown, not at all like the cardinal tuft she had fought so hard to get that eventually fell off and disappeared into nothingness. She knew this crown would last. They were now closer to familiar landmarks: old farmhouses, large barns, connecting fields and meadows, the favorite feasting gardens. This was her home.

"It seems like ages ago since I've been here," she whispered. She didn't know whether it was a good thing or not, because yet another change was coming that she did not want to think about. As they soared in the pale sky, she looked down and recognized the colt from a few weeks ago. A little bit bigger, but the same boisterous youngster she had noticed that particular day. Leah couldn't comprehend all she was witnessing in the colt back then because her thinking had been at low ebb, continually flowing into darkened chambers of her mind. But she understood it now. The colt was free and so was she.

"I can't believe how I can see things so differently now," Leah said. "I know, without a doubt, that I am seeing with good eyes now, just like you taught me, Aquila."

"Good for you, Leah. You've found that the desire to be you inside is now greater than the desire to be something else on the outside. You were so distracted by the way you thought you had to look, what you thought you had to be like, that you almost crashed. But now I know you're going to meet life head on with who you truly are; accepting yourself and accepting all of life around you."

"Yes, you're so right. I remember that colt's mother watching her little one with such love and acceptance, such approval, that it only fueled his amazing frenzy. I believe he was enjoying who he was, accepting himself because he was accepted by love."

"Yes, love is the answer to all of life."

Leah decided right then to let go. She fluidly lifted off of Aquila's back, but promptly shot upwards because of the updraft. Shifting her wings, she regained her flight position. Aquila slowed down to a smooth hover waiting for her to catch up. She maneuvered herself next to him, purposefully getting closer so she could touch his dark golden-brown feathers, his fingers of flight. She compared these giants with her own small brown ones, and this time, she didn't feel inferior. She gratefully felt a clearer acceptance of herself. She wanted to touch the truest essence of who Aquila was; his powerful and majestic being, his electric presence. She had to do this before saying goodbye. Wing tip to wing tip now, she could almost see herself outlined in the same light that she had seen on Aquila as he stood on the fence rail that fateful day when she first laid eyes on him.

"Aquila, the way you looked at me and every time you said my name, I knew it was with love and acceptance. I felt it. You taught me that. But, most of all," Leah continued, faltering at every word, "I felt your heart beat for me…a heartfelt desire to help me…to help me deal…with myself. It has all been…so incredible." She choked as hot tears coursed down her cheeks. "I don't know how I could ever thank you for all you've done for me."

"Sweet Leah," Aquila began, his spirit emitting a light of love to her like a healing salve. "The most wonderful thing I can truly receive from you is seeing you living life, the life you were given and to live it to its fullest. That's where your strength is going to come from every day."

"Well, you certainly have shown me the difference in my own life. Thank you."

"You are very welcome, Leah. I want you to remember what I told you before we began this last trip of ours together."

Leah quickly turned her head so he would not see the tears starting down her face again. Her heart began to ache from sheer agony.

Aquila continued in a gentle, understanding whisper. "I will always be with you, Leah, and I will always carry you. What I mean is that you will always be in my heart and whenever you are in need just think about me and know you are not alone."

"I believe you, Aquila." Nothing was truer, more sure, in her.

Straight ahead, Leah could make out her woods. The day's glow began dimming as the sun made its way toward the horizon. Only a short time left before twilight and too short a time left for her and Aquila. Finally, they were above the pond and nest. Masterfully, Aquila landed on a large, bare limb of a huge oak and sat quietly as Leah circled him until she found a thin twig to perch next to him. The noisy woodland creatures immediately stopped their busyness. They all sensed a different creature of great stature and command among them. Leah was proud to know him, to be with him.

"Do you know why I did that free-falling stunt with you from way up high in the sky?"

She had definitely wondered, but she didn't want to ask anything of this great bird after such a death-defying feat. All she had come to understand was that he was to be trusted.

"No, I don't, Aquila,"

"That free-falling is an eagle couple's flight dance. It's a dance of trust and love for one another. A dance of accepting, of loving, of always being together. Eagle couples stay together for life. So what I did was to symbolize our, yours and mine, staying together for life, Leah, in our spirits. That's why I said I will always be with you, and I meant in the spirit. You have had a great opportunity to have a mountain top experience, and I know you have found it both challenging and exhilarating. But, everyone has to come down from the mountaintop to live in the valley. You will never forget what you've learned up there. You will pass this on to your own little ones and them to theirs, and so forth. For the sprit always lives on. But remember this, Leah—we will never forget this special time together. That is my promise to you."

Leah felt a piercing ache in her heart. She didn't know how she would be able to bear it. Yet, she acknowledged that it was not like the bad heart-hurt she had before arriving to the mountain. With Aquila, it was a good heart-hurt, if one was brave enough to admit it and to bear it. The unavoidable circumstances which bring changes in a life, though unbearable at times, are understandable. Joy does come again in the morning. This special time with Aquila was gone, and there was a future for her to live.

"Leah, when you need strength go to the mountaintop, in your heart, and remember what you there learned from me. When you need peace go to our sacred place, in your heart, above the clouds. And when you feel like love is far away from you think about me, in your heart, and my love will always carry you through."

Leah stared at her enormous friend, enormous in stature of both body and heart. She studied his superb profile as he looked far away toward the east. She noted the beautiful curvature of his beak, the strong brows that hooded his gleaming eyes, and his powerful head; a profound vision of beauty and wisdom. The mountains shined with the glow of final light, settling down on his sacred place as though calling Aquila back to his high home.

"I will never forget you, dearest Leah," Aquila whispered, not turning his head to look at her. With one great swoop into the air he was gone. The branch greatly swayed from the strength of his weight. She watched him meld into the dimming sky. Leah let out a quivering sigh as the warm tears freely trickled down.

"I will never forget you either, dear Aquila," she cried.

She didn't know how long she had remained on the limb staring eastward, deeply hoping to see a glimpse of her Golden Eagle. She closed her eyes as she let her spirit and mind flow in the new gift of peace he had given her. Then she heard it; Aquila's unmistakable call echoing through the clear atmosphere, spiriting straight to her.

Reluctantly, with one last look toward the mountains, Leah flew off the branch, through the trees, and over the fishpond. She heard the cheery song of the toads and peepers. She had missed her home. She almost welcomed their noisome sound, even though one of their kind tried to eat her. She landed on the rim of her nest home.

*It sure seems a long time since I've been home in my woods. But now I'm home safe in my heart, too.*

Leah tidied up her nest from the debris that had landed in it from long absence and neglect. Settling down in it from sheer exhaustion, she let her thoughts carry her to the sacred place far above the white clouds. As evening settled, and looking up into the sky, Leah saw a million sparkling lights shining in the night; a clear testimony and reminder, and proudly so, of her countless Chipping Sparrow ancestors that have lived a good life deemed them on Earth. She could now see with her good eyes that she was one of them.

# Chapter 18

# WELCOME HOME

*Come in the evening, come in the morning;*
*Come when you're looked for, come without warning.*
*- Thomas O. Davis*

"Leah, where have you been? I've been looking all over for you, for days and days. What's been going on? Are you alright?"

Hoozer's excited barrage of questions brought Leah back to the present. She was at the feast garden where the two apple trees were at their end for fruit and readying for the long winter months. The early sun's brilliance rose over the horizon in a red-gold blaze. She welcomed Hoozer's visit wholeheartedly, not having seen her dear House Sparrow friend in a long time. It was vitally important for her to see him now because she had come to cherish all that life had given to her as family and friends.

"Hello, Hoozer! It's so good to see you," Leah exclaimed. Having left with bad feelings the last time they were together, she was ready to make amends. She cringed as she recalled her foul mood directed at him. But, today her spirits were as high as the clouds above that she wished would carry her away to Aquila.

"It's good to see you, too, Leah. It's been a long time since we've been together." Hoozer cleared his throat. "It didn't end very well again with us, did it?"

"No, it didn't, and I'm so sorry."

"No, it was just as much my fault. I'm sorry. I thought I knew better than you did what you wanted or needed. I'm your friend, not your boss. I should have known better."

"Actually, I love you even more as a friend for telling me like it is, Hoozer. You don't know how right you were. I was at the end of my rope, and I wasn't paying much attention. If certain circumstances hadn't happened, I don't think I would have…" Leah stopped talking as tears formed in her eyes.

"What's the matter, Leah? Can I help you?"

"I'm OK. Really I am. It was just what I was thinking about, that's all. But, in reality, I've never felt better in my whole life."

"You know, I could tell something was different about you when I first saw you. I can tell you're at peace. There's something else, too. You look…happy."

"I am, Hoozer. I'm really happy." Leah let out a hardy laugh that caused him to join her. "Have you noticed I don't have any of those crazy feathers on me anymore?"

"Yeah, I noticed. Now you look like the Leah I know."

"Thanks, Hoozer, for always trying to encourage me no matter what awful things I said to you. "You've always been there for me."

"And friends we'll always be."

"There's someone I want to tell you about that will just blow you away. It's the reason I've been gone away for so long and why my life is changed forever. If you liked the story I told you about the origins of my Chipping Sparrow clan, then you'll love this story, too."

"Well, OK, then. Start. I'm all ears."

Leah was pleased at her friend's willingness to listen to her. He had always been a good listener. She almost felt he was one like Aquila, one who saw the world with *good* eyes; always willing to see the good in her. As the Chipping Sparrow watched the House Sparrow get comfortable for the coming narrative, Leah began wondering what he would think about Aquila. Would Hoozer want to meet him? Would Aquila allow it? After all, Aquila was the one that pursued her. She needed Aquila at the exact time he had come into her life. What about Hoozer? Did he need the likes of a great Golden Eagle like she did? For now, all she knew for certain was she was grateful for a great sparrow friend like Hoozer.

The two reconciled friends flew to the topmost point of a nearby giant oak tree and perched on a limb that faced the newborn day. Leah began by pointing toward the direction of the mountain she came to adore.

"A caelis enarrari...the heavens declare: Leah Sparrow is reborn."

CPSIA information can be obtained at www.ICGtesting.com
Printed in the USA
BVOW04s2040090215

387033BV00001B/3/P

9 781498 423083